MAXIM BUTCHENKO

The War Artist

A novel

Translated by

Stephen Komarnyckyj

K L P
Kalyna Language Press Limited

First published in the UK in 2017 by Kalyna Language Press. This paperback edition published in 2017.

Originally Published in Ukraine as Hudožnyk Vojny by Folio (Kharkiv) 2015

Acknowledgements

Cover Design by Aleksey Samovarov

ISBN: 978-0-9931972-8-4

About the Author

Maxim Butchenko, Ukrainian writer and journalist, was born in Donbas (Rovenki city, Luhansk region) in 1977 and lived there until 2012. He began working as a miner and was eventually promoted to assistant site manager.

He moved to Kyiv after completing his higher education and worked as a journalist at the socio-political weekly "Correspondent", which he resigned from after it was bought by oligarch Sergei Kurchenko. During Euromaidan he worked at the magazine "Focus" and later became part of the team of the new weekly, "Novoye Vremya", which became the most influential magazine in Ukraine.

His two novels about the war in Donbas have been published by Folio. In his third novel, which is in preparation for publication, he writes about the women who fought and the fate of soldiers who became disabled.

Butchenko's books have been presented in Lithuania, Poland and France. In 2016, the Czech publisher, Volvox Globator, published The War Artist under the title "Painter of War".

The War Artist is the first novel in a trilogy about the war in Ukraine.

About the Translator

Stephen Komarnyckyj is a poet and translator who was born in Yorkshire, England and maintains strong links with Ukraine, where his family live.

The War Artist

This book is based on real events; its characters are based on genuine people who still live in Donbas.

"I am grateful to Igor Liski and Igor Khasin for their help, which has enabled the translation of this book into English.

I also thank my wife, Tatiana Butchenko, who remains my main source of inspiration and help in my endeavours."

Maxim Butchenko

Foreword

The individual always yearns for freedom. The entire history of humanity is an attempt to describe how to achieve this freedom; how to cast off the chains of oppression. Many ages have passed and we are still struggling to breathe more freely, to live better, to see the world beyond our lives. The individual will always defend these high ideals because our civilisation is built upon them.

In the last days of November 2013 three dozen or so students came to Maidan Nezalezhnosti, Kyiv's central square, their sole demand was that the president sign an association agreement with the EU. President Viktor Yanukovych had previously rejected the plans developed by Ukraine to join the European community; his change of policy resulted in a storm of indignation. Young people gathered on the square and stood peacefully with placards in order to protest his decision; they did not riot or break windows. This peaceful demonstration showed the awareness of younger Ukrainians that they understood their country's place in the world: Ukraine is part of Europe, they are Europeans, they are part of Europe's ancient culture. However, late in the evening of 30 November, this small group was dispersed by the police. Young men and women were beaten with metal truncheons and kicked. It was as if the police were trying to beat the European aspiration out of Ukraine's citizens. The cruel and bloody disposal of a peaceful demonstration and the assault on teenagers with a sincere, albeit naïve, view of their country had a huge impact on the population.

The following day dozens of people gathered on the square. They demanded that the law enforcement officers who had organised the crackdown be held to account. The police also tried to beat and kick the new demonstrators from the square. One week later, one hundred people gathered and the police beat them and tried to crush the peaceful demonstration of popular opinion. Two weeks later there were one thousand people on the square, and one month after that tens of thousands.

During the winter of 2013 to 2014, every day in Kyiv saw a struggle occur between the police and demonstrators. Troops from the interior ministry's special units deployed specialised equipment and sprayed demonstrators with water in temperatures as low as twenty degrees below freezing. The protestors lit bonfires on the square, built barricades and did not surrender.

President Yanukovych wanted to use force to compel people to abandon their European aspirations. He wanted to physically beat the desire to determine their own future out of the people. He was akin to a dictator from the Europe of the nineteen thirties. The police were ordered to fire upon the demonstrators. The number of their victims rapidly increased from ten to several hundred. The name 'The Heavenly Hundred' was given to those people who died on Maidan Nezalezhnosti at the hands of the police. Hundreds of civilians were killed in Ukraine, which is part of Europe, as if it were the Middle Ages. If you visit Kyiv today and go to the square, and walk along Institutska Street, you will see dozens of pictures of the people who died during those months. Young and wholesome, or older and marked with wisdom, those faces stare at you. You need to come and look in their eyes to understand how much they reflect the will and the strong desire for freedom. They were all killed.

More and more people rose in protest with each new death until hundreds of thousands gathered and sang the national anthem, demanding that Yanukovych resign and admit that ordinary citizens had been murdered. They waved the flags of various European countries and the flag of the EU. By February 2014 the popular movement could no longer be restrained. What had begun as student protests now became a popular uprising. President Yanukovych fled Ukraine at the end of February 2014 to avoid being held to account for his actions.

While the western and central areas of the country supported the Maidan protests and their European aspiration, these ideas were not popular in some areas in the east of the country, particularly in Donbas. Large industrial enterprises, mines and factories, including the metallurgical industry, are concentrated in this area. Yanukovych's party, the Party of the Regions, had controlled this area for over a decade.

I was born in Donbas. I worked in a mine and saw the harsh conditions miners laboured in to earn a crust. Every week someone died in the mine and their fellow miners would carry the corpse to the surface; I saw the dead, young faces of those carried past me. The technology used at the mines was at the level of that utilised in the developed world in the nineteen forties and fifties. Furthermore, these enterprises humiliated and abused people, trying to rob them of their dignity. Most of Donbas did not understand the Maidan protest and why it was necessary. *What was the aim of overthrowing the president, even if his hands were smeared with blood?*

Russia successfully exploited this mood. Their leadership, as personified in Vladimir Putin, annexed Crimea. The Russian government then decided to split Ukraine. In order to do this Russia intimidated the population of Donbas by using propaganda primarily distributed by the TV channels. The population of Donbas feared that radicals from the Kyiv Maidan would come and slaughter everyone in the east. The absurdity of these accusations is obvious because the main slogan of the protestors in Kyiv was European values. Russian special intelligence units soon began to arrive in Donbas. They provoked mass demonstrations and seized police and security-service buildings.

The Kyiv government quickly lost control over Donbas. So called Cossacks, military, non-government organisations, simultaneously entered Donbas from Russia. These Cossacks took advantage of the weakness of the Ukrainian government after Yanukovych had fled. They began to seize entire cities. Ukraine, weakened after the rule of a president with dictatorial tendencies, was almost torn into two separate parts. One part comprised Crimea, captured by Russian special forces, and Donbas, where Russian military organisations and the Russian army battled against the Ukrainian military. The other part, the vast majority of Ukraine, remained under the control of its government.

My book begins at the end of the Euromaidan revolution. Its heroes are two brothers who are on opposing sides of the conflict. One supports Ukraine, which has chosen a European course, the other does not understand why that is necessary. They are opposites, like light and dark, but sometimes the darkness is not utterly dark. This book is, in effect, a true story based on my relatives. I saw many of the things that happened in the lives of these brothers. I can only record them and replay their fate in this book. How could such a large war with missiles and Howitzers be possible in the centre of Europe? Why have ten thousand people been killed, and who is to blame? What happens to a family when two brothers become bitter enemies? This book tells us about Ukraine's past and warns of future dangers. It tells us that the desire for freedom is stronger than the fear of death.

Translator's Foreward - An English Perspective

The War that Europe Forgot…

What makes a man betray his country? Maxim Butchenko's novel, The War Artist, explores this question against the backdrop of a war forgotten by Europe. As I write this introduction, in February 2017, shells are raining down on a city in Adviivka; a European city. A twenty-four year old ambulance driver has been killed overnight after a Russian shell landed next to his vehicle. Civilians huddle in tents, in temperatures of minus twenty degrees celsius, and around field kitchens where the Ukrainian army doles out hot food.

Nolan Peterson, an ex-US Special Forces' pilot-turned-journalist, says he has never seen fighting as intense as he has witnessed in Ukraine. Russia currently deploys more tanks in Donbas than there are in the entire Czech, French and German armies combined. The war has claimed ten thousand casualties by some estimates, however, a German intelligence report, which emerged in February 2015, gave a figure of fifty thousand; yet the conflict is often misunderstood, largely due to Russia's ability to influence western media by distributing stories through manipulated journalists and corrupt politicians.

Donbas, in eastern Ukraine, is a vast rolling expanse of Steppe where the horizon is broken by collieries and slag heaps. Miners work with primitive equipment and are often maimed and killed. The area was the site of what Luhansk native Maxim Butchenko calls a soviet experiment after the second world war. Cities were built according to a strict soviet model and miners, often ex-convicts, were shipped in from across the Soviet Union. Some areas retained a Ukrainian identity but many became soulless enclaves of Marxist-Leninism. After the Soviet Union collapsed, the area became a kind of wild east where organised crime flourished. Business rivals were assassinated and crime bosses donned lounge suits and posed as ordinary businessmen while sending thugs in ski masks to beat up or kill their enemies. Oligarchs with shadowy pasts soon owned the areas' mines and industries.

In 2004, Victor Yanukovych won the presidential election and huge crowds took to the streets in Kyiv to protest against massive voter fraud (including multiple voting by the same people and support from dead voters) and the result was cancelled. Yanukovych tried to organise his own demonstrations. He and his cronies bused in miners from Donbas; they were told that the rest of Ukraine was fascist. The soviet mind-set, which had survived in Donbas, had fossilised like the coal beneath its vast plains. Its inhabitants were only too willing to believe the fairy tale of the fascists ruling Kyiv. Yanukovych lost the subsequent re-run, but despite massive evidence of fraud he and his cronies were never prosecuted.

He won the presidential election in 2010, but Yanukovych soon tore off the mask of a slick technocrat and quickly imposed, perhaps, the most corrupt regime in history on Ukraine. During 2010 to 2013, businesses were seized by a small gang of his cronies, collectively known as 'The Family'. State tenders were won by companies ultimately linked to him or his entourage and opposition politicians were jailed on bogus charges. Ukrainians, however, believed that he would keep his promise to sign an association agreement with the EU. They thought that he would have to hold fair elections to have any credibility with the European Union.

When Yanukovych refused to sign the agreement in 2013, students demonstrated on Maidan Nezalezhnosti, Kyiv's main square. They knew now that Yanukovych would try to stay in power indefinitely and loot the country. He sent thugs in uniform to crush the protests. Activists were kidnapped and murdered, or died under sniper fire.

Yanukovych ultimately fled the country with the

aid of his patron, Putin, in March 2014. Russia sent Special Forces into Crimea in 2014 and organised a fake referendum to legitimise its occupation. Special Forces went into Donbas and seized public buildings. There were already demonstrations organised by Yanukovych's Party of the Regions; they whipped together crowds of workers from their enterprises as they tried to hold on to power in a region they regarded as their own personal bailiwick.

Russia was able to recruit some of these workers into hybrid forces, comprising a mixture of locals and Russian mercenaries. They set up two pseudo republics, the DNR and the LNR, in Donetsk and Luhansk; fake countries created by Russian intelligence and its deniable assets, led by shadowy characters. The hybrid army was used as cannon fodder by the regular Russian army, who were in Ukraine from 2014 onwards, despite the brazen lies of the Kremlin. There is no genuine separatist movement in Ukraine; there is the Russian army. There are some Ukrainians and multi-national mercenaries in Russian-led units.

Russia had hoped to split Ukraine apart in 2014, believing that many people across southern and eastern Ukraine would flock to their banner. This operation, known as the 'Russian Spring', failed dismally because Ukrainians remained loyal to their state and understood Putin's kleptocracy only too well. Russia was left occupying only part of Donbas.

Maxim Butchenko's novel begins at the point where Russian Special Forces are seizing buildings and destabilising Luhansk. It is a glimpse into a mining community torn apart by a war in which brothers and sisters, parents and children are often split apart by the front line. It exposes how Russia has inflamed the conflict and used bamboozled locals as a cover for its invasion.

The book explores what motivates someone to betray his country, in a non-judgemental manner, by the character of

Anton Nedelkov, a miner whose dreams of becoming a painter are frustrated.

At the moment the war is a destination. You can sit on a café veranda in Kyiv and watch the wind flurry your cappuccino, then catch a train hundreds of miles east to the combat zone. The miners live in poverty, while criminals cruise the streets in *Bentleys*. Many people only know of the world outside through media outlets controlled by oligarchs. This world seems as remote and unreal as if seen through the wrong end of a telescope.

This book is a glimpse into Ukraine's present but also into one potential future for the western world. We stand at a crossroads and must choose wisely or we will end up like Anton, in darkness deeper than that congealed within the fossil coal of Donbas.

Chapter One

In Luhansk, separatists have seized the SBU building, and broken doors and windows.

From the Vostochnyi Variant newspaper, 06.04.2014

In Luhansk, armed separatists have issued an ultimatum and said that if their demands are not met they will openly confront the authorities. This statement was made in a video distributed by the individuals who seized the SBU building in the city: "We, the joint staff of the army of the South-East, appeal to the people of our provinces thus: if our demands are not met we will openly confront the authorities. The building where the province's SBU is based is completely under our control. Our army has grown. We are ready to deploy a reserve squad in Donetsk if required." The separatists reported.

From an item on the UNN site, 07.04.2014

A middle-aged man, who was generally known as Petrovych but whose passport gave his name as Kolia Chernyshev, spat with relish on the pavement and clicked the cancel button on his mobile phone. His sombre face, which might have been carved with an axe, was grimaced in bewilderment. Kolia, or Petrovych, stood on the corner of a street which bore the name, as was traditional in Donbas, of Moskovskaya. Private residential buildings with grey, and in places cracked, slates resembled old turtles who had crawled here to stand in long, deep lines for some reason. The row of turtles was heading sideways, towards where it seemed they would die. A wooden fence stretched alongside the houses, through the apertures of which the courtyards were visible. This was the outskirts of Rovenky, a provincial mining settlement. The local population mainly worked in a number of mines, the market, and small, two or three person businesses.

Petrovych was returning home after a shift at one of the mines when he received a telephone call. The call had troubled him so much that a minute after it had ended he spat on the fence of his own property. His heart was so deeply troubled that he scared the two dogs in his yard, who seemed to understand every word uttered by their master and barked deafeningly into the emptiness. Trampling briefly on the spot, he was gathering himself to enter the yard when his neighbour, Anton Nedelkov, emerged from the house next door. He was a thirty-year old, skinny man, with a large, bulging nose. Anton purposefully headed to the nearest kiosk to buy cigarettes.

"Hey neighbour, have you heard? The Banderites have dispatched a column of nationalists to the town, they want to butcher the men and set the women to work in the fields. There is a meeting at the crossroads, many people are going," Kolia blurted out these words as he gesticulated vigorously. He expected his neighbour to respond with a selection of expletives used in the Steppe and to be shocked; or even, perhaps, pass out.

After the ex-president, Viktor Yanukovych, had fled Ukraine and parliament became the sole legitimate government body in the country, a wave of meetings swept Donbas. Initially, they had a peaceful character and were often organised by leaders of Yanukovych's 'Party of the Regions'. They aimed to show Kyiv that it was too soon to write them off. However, in Luhansk and Donetsk, mobs, numbering in the thousands, seized the SBU's, police's and prosecutors' buildings. It subsequently became known that armed sabotage and intelligence units of the GRU, Russian military intelligence, had in fact stormed these buildings. The Ukrainian military then launched the anti-terrorist operation. The main theatre of action was Donetsk province, but in small towns in the Luhansk area terrified residents waited daily for the coming of the national guard.

These rumours agitated the whole area more than if a plague had been sweeping the Steppe and annihilating every living thing.

So Petrovych, with the blind faith of a woodpecker, hammered these terrible predictions into his neighbour. Anton did not fall into hysterics or cry, *Anyone who can must save themselves,* instead he calmly said, "Go and get some sleep, Kolia," understandingly, and turned his back on his neighbour.

The word 'sleep' induced some oscillations in Petrovych's internal world, similar to the vibrations created by the tapping of a hammer. Five minutes later he had convinced his neighbour that Kyiv had dispatched a military force to Rovenky to seize the town; the inhabitants of which would then be replaced by Ukrainians from Prykarpattia. Petrovych concluded his threatening speech regarding the dark future of Rovenky by striking his fence so forcefully that a chunk of wood broke off and hit a window in his house.

"So, do you see how screwed up everything is, do you?" he almost yelled, his eyes smouldering like a capelin tossed on a griddle.

Anton slowly moved his gaze from his neighbour's wide, glaring eyes on to the fence and the broken glass and thought about how this was a sign. Anton believed in signs and omens. He found, within his boring provincial life, traces, inchoate shapes, that always led him to new things. On the path of life that was lain across the bright yellow Steppe, covered with dry grass, he strove to find some verdant patch of green meadow. Now he nodded in agreement with Petrovych, *Yes, they would go to the meeting.*

Twenty minutes later, they were already at the Diakovskyi crossroads, which led into the town. A few dozen protestors were standing there and partly blocking the road. There were a couple of old men, old women in gaudy headscarves, drunken men, and an amply proportioned woman bearing a green-bottomed frying pan.

From morning onwards, the local TV station, *NIKA-TV*, had broadcast announcements regarding the expected arrival of the Ukrainian military and asked all who were not indifferent to gather on the road leading out of the town. Some had organised buses, some travelled independently, and now they all crowded slightly to the side of the road. Only the most despairing stood in the middle, staring into the distance like the heroic warriors in tales of yore when people awaited the advent of the Tatar-Mongol horde.

One such hero, a heavily inebriated and long-unshaven man, with dark shadows and the coal dust of a miner around his eyes, waved his arms as if directing traffic. This 'hero' had the somewhat un-epic name of Mitia Zakharov and, although under sixty years old, he was already receiving his pension, but still worked out of habit. There were dozens like him in the town; they worked at the coal face or on the tunnels into the coal seam; after twenty years they were pensioned off according to the primary list of particularly hazardous occupations. They did not abandon the mines and were assigned to lighter, unskilled mining work.

Now, as he stood on the road, Mitia felt like a primary lister; he was struggling with a cough, a hangover, and the incessant movement of cars. And the Banderites, unfortunately, seemed stubbornly reluctance to enter his decaying town. He menaced some unseen person in the distance with a fist covered in curved stripes of stubborn coal dust. Then, profoundly agitated, he left his post, joined the crowd and immediately seized the microphone. "Comrades, I want to say," he began hoarsely, but did not have time to complete the phrase. The woman with the frying pan grabbed the microphone and, with comic despair, yelled that the inhabitants of Rovenky must immediately stop the 'brown plague' moving-in on the town.

The inebriated Mitia wanted to continue his ardent

appeal to his comrades and tried to reclaim the microphone from the frying pan-wielding orator, however, the ample woman with her finely attuned senses had rumbled him. She unexpectedly swung her kitchen utensil with improbable swiftness and 'accidentally' caught the drunkard on his chin. The blow, which had all her force behind it, laid him out on the asphalt.

"Hey people, look at this, he's fainted, he couldn't endure the stress," the ample woman formulated her excuse, even as her inebriated victim was falling. "The Banderites want to lay us all out like that."

Anton smiled slyly because this scene imbued the war, with its mythical enemy moving towards the town, with a comical feel. Most of the people rallying were unemployed or pensioners. It looked like the guardian angel of all those fifty or older, with nothing to do, had decided to gather them in one place as an 'interested group'. They had, like dominoes, swung into the passageways of the buildings, impelling their agitation to others who had just been standing around and smoking, and the most desperate were intending to throw themselves into the path of enemy tanks.

As Anton was about to leave, a heavy-set man, with a St. George's Ribbon in the buttonhole of his black jacket and a baseball bat in his hand, leaped to the microphone. His hair was tied in a Japanese-style pigtail. "When they come, let's deal with them as they dealt with the Berkut on the Maidan," the aficionado of Japanese hairstyling yelled. The crowd buzzed like a disturbed beehive. "I say to you, let's take an elementary Molotov cocktail and throw it at them, just like they, sod it, threw them at our Berkut," the big, baseball bat-wielder continued. "I say to you, let's take bottles and petrol and burn, burn, burn them! What else can I say? What more is there to say? Let's do it!"

Talk of Molotov cocktails had thrilled the mob.

Someone yelled that they needed to build barricades and the old ladies proclaimed that they must organise a religious procession against the evil Maidan and drive Satan hence with Holy Water. Mitia, finally recovering, snatched the microphone from another bellowing old man who was recollecting how 'the German boots had reeked as they trampled the soil of Rovenky'.

"Comrades, I want to say," he said hoarsely, gazing around. He faltered momentarily before continuing in a more eloquent voice, "Comrades, comrades, let's sober up before we gather again."

The crowd continued to buzz, but it was getting dark and the demonstration soon deflated like a balloon. Anton tried to find Petrovych's eyes, but his neighbour chanced to be elsewhere in the crowd. They needed to go back home. The twilit haze was a soft brush, gradually blurring faces, trees and the sign announcing Rovenky. The remaining figures wandered along the road like the shades of their ancestors who had gone to fight fascism seventy-three years ago. These shadows now roamed the dense spring air, finding no solace.

Chapter Two

Luhansk city council deputies demand amnesty for the individuals who seized the SBU building. The deputies state that: "We need to grant Russian the status of a second state language via legislation as soon as possible and end this stand off once and for all. We are one people and the artificial degradation of the language issue cannot divide us. The most important thing is to prevent bloodshed." They believe that, 'the inhabitants of Luhansk stand against any manifestations of radicalism and extremism, however worthy their objectives may be. They are tired of the constant upheavals, they want stability, faith in tomorrow, and confidence in their personal safety and that of their nearest and dearest.'

From an item on the Podrobnosti site, 11.04.2014

Anton crossed the threshold of his house in the early evening, but suddenly realised he had forgotten to buy any cigarettes. Sighing angrily, he was heading resolutely back to the kiosk when his younger daughter, Diana, ran to meet him. He broke into a smile involuntarily. Diana raised her hand to her father, who picked her up like a toy; how she had grown in the three years that had passed since she was born.

On the day Diana appeared in his life he had returned from Luhansk utterly desiccated; he felt as if only a fraction of the water in his body remained. It was the day of his third and last attempt to enter the fine arts faculty of the T. Shevchenko Luhansk National University. All his attempts to become a professional artist ended when he had again failed to pass the examination.

He had been skilled at drawing and painting since his childhood, and his first, truly well-crafted landscape was executed when he was ten years old. It depicted the deep lemon-yellow of the Steppe and the soft rolling hills, which seemingly pressed together and stretched to the horizon; in the distance, sunset, speckles of light, blazed on the dark pyramid of a slag heap. It was an unusual painting.

Anton, like all children, messed around, roamed, and was disobedient. Getting him to sit at a table was not a simple business. However, once he began sketching, he could not stop until he had completed his work. His father would look at his picture, then at the slim, curly haired Anton, sitting placidly at the table and sketching the outlines of his next creation, and say nothing. Within that long silence were concentrated all the unrealised hopes of Anton's father. He would ruffle his son's hair and say, "You are like me." Twenty years had passed, but Anton still remembered the words as clearly as if they had been uttered that same evening. In truth, it was only long afterwards that he realised the deeper meaning of that paternal phrase.

"Papa, papa, why are you silent?" The words uttered by little Diana brought Anton back to reality. He shook his head as he tried to flick away his thoughts as if they were cigarette ash.

"Daughter, your dad thinks it's sometimes useful to be quiet," he chuckled.

Liuba, his wife, entered. She was a well-built woman with a worn-out face. Without saying a word she picked up her daughter and took her into another room, closing the door behind her. They had not spoken for five days. *Although, was today the fifth day?*

The couple had met after his first attempt to enter the university. They had gone to a few bars and, the by now half-cut, Anton had told her his story about how, since he was a child, he had dreamed of becoming a painter, exhibiting his work in the capital, and earning a living from his art. Liuba nearly choked on her beer, "What art? You have to go to work in the mine. How else can you earn a living in this town?"

Anton could not answer that question then and it was pointless to try. Two months after this discussion she had become pregnant, and four months later they were married. He remembered the moment when they had stood in the one-storey village council building in Klenovyi. The young couple had lacked the money to get married in the city's registry office. That would have cost two hundred hrynyas, but here it was possible to get hitched for eighty kopecks. The chair of the village council was a stout woman, who was dressed in a long, gaudy dress decorated with wilted red-rag roses. She declared them man and wife solemnly, with a hint of anguish, as if she regretted the loss of her own youth. Then she pushed the button on the tape recorder and Mendelssohn's *Wedding March* broke, or rather banged, out. The young couple looked startled at the chair, whose towering hairstyle resembled *The Ninth Wave* of Ivan Aivazovsky. The whole ceremony consisted of three people in one room.

In the evening there was the family celebration at his mother-in-law's home, where parents, sisters and uncles gathered. Anton sat at the head of the table, hugging that now fairly broad part of Liuba's body, which in other, non-pregnant, women might have been called a waist. Nineties music thundered out, various salads jolted to the beat of the rhythm, empty bottles lined up like spent cartridge cases, and the bride's sister ogled the newly weds.

Anton's mother sat in her chair, as sad as her son, and looked around as he added his new wife to the family. The groom's brother, Sergei, stood by the entrance to the room and looked over the guests a little squeamishly. It was impossible to tell that the men were brothers by any visual characteristics. Anton was tall with curly hair and hard, regular, angular features. Sergei was of medium height with a softly delineated face and a nose that resembled a goose's beak. There were five years between them, but occasionally it felt like fifty.

During their childhood, in the yard of the building where they had lived, they often fought each other or with boys from the neighbouring yard. Sergei had watched over his brother, but had rarely intervened in his childhood. On the contrary, instead of protecting Anton, it was often Zheniu, a neighbour living near them on the square, he had looked after. Sergei never sought an answer to this and never even asked himself why this was the case.

The brothers were separated by a line of disengagement. Their familial proximity bore an unconscious character, as if someone had imposed the sense of relationship. It was not engendered in the depths of their souls; this fraternal difference bore them, for an extended period, in opposing directions. It was hard even to remember their mutual games on the streets. Once they had squirted water out of bottles at each other and their whole apartment had been saturated. Their mother was out at the shop and when she returned she gasped in shock, grabbed a belt and chased Sergei.

"It wasn't my idea," he yelled at her. "It's not my fault," he explained, cowering behind the bathroom door, "Anton started it."

"Open up, I'll give you Anton," their mother yelled, "you're older, you need to have your head screwed on." She clattered on the door. Meanwhile, the younger brother was hiding under the bed.

Their differences could be seen at the wedding, with both brothers occupying different corners of the room. The guests stomped along to yet another song about unrequited love, and the neighbour's cat, Tusia, carefully roamed the empty chairs, trying to pull a morsel of happiness from the table with her muddy paw.

The new family's first day began to the accompaniment of the deafening, nasal-snorted breaths of the young, still sleeping wife. Anton woke and grasped his head, which was sliced apart with pain. The larger part of the bed was occupied with the hefty, pregnant body of his new wife. He looked around.

The wedding presents were in a corner of the room: a bright red and blue dinner service, a couple of blankets, a painting depicting a half-naked, skinny girl against the backdrop of the great pyramids, a set of Chinese cooking knives, and a bunch of flowers clearly plucked from the garden next door.

The couple spent half of the day collapsed in their bed and decided to have a stroll in the evening. Liuba pulled on her flowered dress, with difficulty, over her large, rounded shoulders. She sat before the mirror, separated from Anton by a palisade of cheap cosmetics, daubs of nail varnish in various blood-coloured hues, and an unopened bottle of champagne she had brought back from the evening party. The dress snagged on her heavy bust and was reluctant to descend further. Liuba grunted. Her bare thighs shook hopelessly with her impatient efforts. Her hands dragged the dress downwards, but the fabric halted stubbornly, without reaching her waist.

Anton lay on the dishevelled bed and watched how Liuba, with despairing tenacity, tried to drag on the dress. The spectacle amused him as he watched this half-naked woman contentedly, without the least sexual arousal. It was like the completion of a symbolic act, a striving to return to the dimensions of her past when, still quite slender, she had strolled the street and teenagers had wolf-whistled at her. The unequal struggle continued, but the dress held its ground. Finally, the exhausted woman swore, sat on the bed and sighed resignedly. The dress hung haplessly on her broad, perspiring back, like a flag of surrender in the battle for youth. Anton sighed and helped Liuba pull the ill-fated garment over her head. She looked thankfully at him and he saw a curious mixture of genuine grief, tenderness and hurt in her blue eyes. Anton would see that look several times during his life.

An awkward, but extremely brief, pause ensued. Liuba turned away from her husband, panting quietly. She pulled on another dress, which was black with white polka dots, much broader than the other one, and resembled a shabby bathrobe. It covered her body immediately, like a cover thrown over a car. She stood before the mirror twisting her broad backside, inspecting her back and pursing her lips tightly with regret. She did not like herself. Then she sighed again, but this time it was more deeply, as if from the depths of her soul. She spent another minute twisting before the mirror, painted her lips with a thick layer of blood-red lipstick and sprayed herself with cheap deodorant. The pungent floral fumes covered her and everything in the hallway, even reaching Anton, who was sitting on a chair in the kitchen and smoking.

A few seconds later she blurted out that it was time to go. During those days they lived in a rented apartment on the top floor of a nine-storey building and the lift had not worked since the mid-nineties. In order to leave the building they had to traipse down half a kilometre of stairs.

"I'm ready now. Do I look okay?" she asked, turning towards him. He looked her over from head to foot. She looked much older than her twenty-four years. Her eyes were already wrinkling with age; the spacious dress could not completely cover her ample figure, and the gaudily daubed cosmetics only emphasised her fatigued age. But Anton did not notice any of this because he loved her.

"You are beautiful and other men will be jealous of me," he said, smiling softly.

"And you just look into my eyes so you are not repelled by the rest of me," she said, either in jest or seriously, and also smiled softly.

They went along the darkened street to the Dubok bar. Anton supported his ungainly wife by the elbow and it was obvious he was unused to female company. He had not been involved in a long-term romantic relationship before he had met her because he always struggled to strike up a conversation with a woman. Iryna, his mother, had introduced him to Liuba, who was a very distant relative. She had seen how her son lacked female affection and decided to bring them together by inviting them to her birthday party. She would live to regret her action, and her inability to separate them, for the rest of her life. This anguish had a beginning but no end. It was only much later that Anton would understand his mother's view.

As usual, the bar was crowded that evening and reeked of the shashlik kebabs that were cooking in its yard. An inebriated singer with a hoarse voice took to the stage and sang about how she was sitting in a sports car heading somewhere. She wielded a guitar, the synthesiser emitted one hundred beats per minute and the drunken customers shook their beer-bellies between the tables, seemingly dancing.

Anton and his wife sat near the passage to the toilets, which happened to be on the street and were contained in a wooden cubicle. Liuba turned on her stool and watched with interest as two drunkards at the next table argued about what the 'Oranges', who were in power, were up to. The dispute was protracted in proportion to the two bottles of wine they had drunk.

"So, who are these Oranges? They are westerners unable to work, all off to Poland and Germany. And what have they done for the country?" One of the drinkers waved a hand which held a lighted cigarette.

"You can't say that. I've been in Prykarpattia. All the houses are clean and well kept, oh, Lord, even spitting on the ground is shameful," the other replied.

"What, are you with the Banderites?" the first one replied, striking the table with his fist in front of his opponent. Cigarette ash soared into the air and, as if purposefully, descended into a glass which still contained some wine.

An awkward pause followed. The man with the cigarette looked into his glass, trying to scoop out the ash with his finger, clearly to no avail. He turned his head from the table and spat on the floor, then downed the ash and wine mixture in a single gulp. The other man smiled, watching his unfortunate friend, and both of them forgot what they were talking about. It would all have finished peacefully if Liuba had not intervened.

"Does this mean that your friend doesn't support Donbas?" she thundered, so that both the imbibers looked at her. Anton wanted to urge his wife not to get involved, but she did not give him a chance. "Don't you understand that he is a traitor?" Liuba continued to point at the man who had been in Prykarpattia.

At that moment the melody of the song, *Potomu Chto nelzya byt na svete krasyvoj takoj*, subsided and silence filled the bar. The man with the cigarette looked suspiciously at Liuba, then at his comrade. It seemed a fight was about to start, but it was not clear who he would swipe, Anton's wife or the defender of the 'Oranges'.

"Guys, she's joking, chill," said Anton, trying to defuse the situation.

"Why do you think I'm joking? No, I'm serious, let him answer who he is for, ours or the Banderites," Liuba insisted. Her face was determined, as if she had decided that this question was now of the utmost importance. The man with the cigarette frowned. The other rose slightly. Anton sweated, and the atmosphere was tense and electric. "Let him say what he thinks," Liuba insisted.

"Can't you just be quiet, is it that hard?" Anton blurted at her, but it was too late to extinguish the conflict.

"So, I should be quiet?" Liuba responded, directing her fury at her husband. "Let the bastard answer for his words."

Anton tried to be self effacing because the men had already forgotten about their fight and were now focused on Liuba. "Liuba, I'm just asking you to be quiet. Let them sort it out."

"Yes, you backed off. Why are you scared? He's a traitor.

And what are you, knob-head, sitting there, you can't handle the heat," Liuba yelled at her husband. Her further words were drowned out by another sparkling ditty about unrequited love.

A young waiter in jeans and a red jacket approached the table in the midst of the uproar and asked them what they would like to order.

The man with the cigarette grinned and his friend laughed. "You've landed yourself with a right cow there; she'll screw with your head," he said contemptuously, and spat again.

The chorus of songs about broken love drowned out Liuba's angry muttering and the ridicule of the neighbouring table. The blaring music and the simple, senseless words absorbed something imperceptible to those around Anton. Something profound, almost anguished; the weight of his disappointment, the pain of misunderstanding, a vague awareness of his predicament. All this departed from the confused soul of Anton with a single breath.

Chapter Three

According to the 0642.ua site, in the centre of Alchevsk (Luhansk Province), on Saturday 5 April, a meeting for the 'Russian Spring' took place. The site notes that the people at the meeting behaved hesitantly and could not explain precisely why they had gathered. Calls for nationalisation and social equality were made from an improvised stage. The culmination of the meeting was to have been the raising of the Russian flag. However, the protestors raised something resembling a French flag while chanting, "Russia, Russia!"

One week later and Anton was already working at the mine, but he had to undergo two months of training before he could go down the pit. The route there began with donning miner's apparel: boiler suit, leggings and rubber boots. Pulling on his helmet sideways, he ventured into the changing room with a long row of cubicles, like wardrobes, with chargers for the mining lamps.

Beneath the cubicles were deep recesses for breathing apparatuses, which were cylindrical objects weighing one and a half kilograms. In the event of a conflagration in the mine, fire and smoke would spread quickly through the narrow shafts and ventilation system, and a miner would have to engage his life preserver, fit its breathing tube and put on goggles; if not, they faced an agonising death from suffocation. Sometimes a miner did not fit the apparatus properly and it did not work. The contorted bodies of miners who were not near breathing apparatus had been found after many fires. The apparatus was very heavy, so they often stowed it in the mine workings or by the surface entrance.

On receiving his miner's lamp, respirator and breathing apparatus, Anton headed to a crowded area before the lift. It consisted of a crate on a rope attached to a winding machine.

The miners referred to the first descent into the mine as 'the wedding night'. At that moment everything they had known before changed. The surface and the mine were two opposing concepts for them, like the sea and dry land for a sailor, or the air and earth for a pilot. This conception is forever implanted in the soul of a miner, whether they are working or not.

"Let's speed it up lads." The new recruits were urged on by a lift operator long past her youth. She checked that they all entered the cage, and would give the signal for going up or down. The men all whinged like street cats miaowing at their mother.

"The main thing is that the rope isn't torn, if that happens they'll be scraping us off the walls," a youth covered with acne uttered vigorously.

"Don't worry, they'll send others," chuckled their instructor.

They all prepared themselves as the operator gave the signal. Anton's virginal conception of life broke at the moment the cage hurtled sharply downwards for almost one kilometre into the depths. His ears lay flat, his legs trembled from the shift in his weight, and his body braced itself for the impact. The cage seemingly fell downwards into the innards of some giant creature; an ancient dragon born when life had just appeared on the earth. They fell, bypassing its nasopharynx and oesophagus, and would be shattered when they reached its stomach. But the cage now descended softly and the miners eased out of it as sweetly as sprats from a jar.

Ahead of them there was a menacing outline, a black hole. It seemed that as the figures went deeper they disappeared and the light from their lamps illuminated hazy lumps. This atavistic, primal fear of the darkness would always haunt the miners; even when they had grown accustomed to the obscurity, the fear of the unknown would always linger. Perhaps that is why so many of the mine workers visit the bar for a few drinks after a shift and drink to excess so that unconscious fear can be consigned to oblivion.

However, for Anton, the first day at the mine was devoted to studying. He passed through mine workings with a group of new-starters and they were heading back to the lift. As they returned they saw, in the depths of the workings, a smallish, one and a half ton wagon that had come off the rails. As the miners say, it had 'stalled'. One of the workers was labouring with the aid of a prop (typically this was a piece of pine) as a lever. He stuck one end of the wood under the wheels and planted his whole body on the other. By doing this he managed to raise the wagon by a few centimetres. Meanwhile, his partner placed the wheels on the rail and that was it, the wagon was almost sorted. But at that moment the thirty-five year old miner, who was holding the lever, slipped. The lever whacked him on the knee with all the force of the weight it bore. The rumbling of the descending wagon accompanied the deafening screams of the injured man. His kneecap had shattered with the impact, as if it were just a piece of French bread. Everyone rushed to help him. Anton and a wrinkled, grey-haired old miner pulled the traumatised man, who was now on a stretcher, to the lift.

"This is your first day then?" the old man asked, and without waiting for a reply continued, "down the mine it's the same as being on the front line in the war. If you're not killed, you're crippled."

Anton remembered that old man's words more than once.

His real working life began after that day. He was a labourer at first and placed the wagon wheels on the rails, dragged the wood and ensured the conveyor belt did not collapse through being overloaded with coal. Once, during a night shift, he sat on the distributor, a structure made of welded sheet-metal resembling a drain pipe; it was designed to pour coal from one conveyor to another. The engines hummed steadily and the darkness covered everything. Anton sat with his back leaned against the cutter and the light of his mining lamp captured the stream of coal from among the darkness as it crunched, rumbled and fell from the distributor.

The nocturnal hours are particularly hard for miners and it was around four o'clock in the morning when Anton felt a strong urge to sleep. His body ceased battling against fatigue. The monotonous noise of the conveyor belt and the pouring sound of the coal became a lullaby. Anton collapsed so swiftly into the arms of Morpheus that he did not have time to say to himself, *sleeping in the mine isn't allowed.*

If he was caught he would be fired. Every shift in the mine workings was overseen by engineers who ensured the work was done; they were called the 'Sixth Directorate'. The name was taken from the KGB's 'Sixth Directorate', who had been responsible for economic counter intelligence and preventing industrial espionage in the soviet era. The miners named these engineers 'KGB men' and had a painfully strong aversion to them.

Anton plunged into his nocturnal dream, oblivious to the danger of being caught. *He was in the Steppe. Hills burned with summer and rolled in waves to the horizon. Bare shrubs formed ragged blotches over the nearby pasture. A row of poplars stood to the right. A ribbon of dirt road, which looked as if someone had just cast it on the surface of the Steppe, lay to the left. It rose and fell with the undulations of the ground. Dark clouds loomed ominously over the plain. A few scant sun-rays trickled thinly through their grey carapace. He stood on a small hillock and looked towards the trees. The cool breeze caressed his face with its coarse hands. He had to go somewhere. Anton felt the need to walk as you do when you need to blunt some deep heartache.* Motion does more than just change the landscape around you; it renders the flow of life visible; its unstoppable momentum breaks the sense of an impasse.

Anton wanted to tell himself where he needed to go, but he could not. It felt as if someone choked him so he could not utter any sound. The sense that he could not control his body troubled him and engulfed his whole being. Panic pierced his innards, then spread through his chest. The feeling of hopelessness, multiplied by a fear of the unknown, captured him. He grunted despairingly and ran down the hill. When he had made only a half metre of ground his foot snagged on a cobblestone and he fell stretched out. His face was immersed in the arid soil. He rolled on to his back, gasping. Clouds of ash shunted over the sky and piled on top of each other. The wind tore dark sulphurous chunks from their edges. The sight enchanted him. Anton forgot his fear momentarily and gazed into the sky. He watched these ash monsters who assaulted the neighbouring clouds; they wanted to devour but also often just fled their foes.

"It's like a dream," he said, with no surprise at the return of his ability to talk. He watched this ethereal battle for a few minutes more and, having inspected it thoroughly, tried to rise. He felt a heaviness around his stomach, as if someone had tied him to a heavy object. He got to his knees laboriously and could not rise another centimetre. The weight was now somewhere inside himself.

"Bloody hell, this can't be happening, I'm probably sick, maybe I have a tumour," he said to himself. He made another attempt to stand and, conquering himself, grunted and rose. Hunched and gripping his abdomen, he lurched along the road. Anton probed around his body and suddenly realised that his gut had increased in size and even protruded somewhat from under his shirt. He explored its convex surface with his fingers and heard someone tapping on the walls of his stomach from inside. Anton was scared again, his whole body trembled and he tried to rip this alien thing from his body. Then a vast calm and hazy tranquillity descended on him.

"It's a boy," he said, smiling.

Moving forward was no longer so hard. He shunted along the road, occasionally casting his head upwards to look at the passing clouds. Then, when he felt unusually invigorated again, an unexpected and savage pain twisted in his stomach as if someone had pierced it with a sharp object and rolled it hither and thither. It's all over now, he thought and in a fit of suffering threatened the sky with his fist. When the pain had reached its utmost limit, almost compelling him to lose consciousness, he felt something loosen in his stomach. He touched it with his hands. Coal chunks as black as pitch fell out of him, as if his stomach were cleaved in two and a stream of coal gushed forth. Agony savaged his body again; he stood in the middle of the road with a pile of coal forming before him. Unable to endure any more, Anton yelled at the heavens to the one who sits there, imploring their help. That cry was cast towards those ashen monsters in the sky. They seemed to beat it aside with their paws and laughed thunderously at the little man amid the Steppe.

They would have continued for a long time, but suddenly everything stopped. His stomach closed. The flow halted and the cloud monsters were calm, as if nothing had happened, like waves basking in blue waters. Anton fell to his knees, breathing deeply, and it seemed to him that he hawked up small chunks of coal. He vomited for a few minutes.

The first thing he saw when the convulsions subsided was the large pile of coal in the road. In a second he realised that something had come out of his stomach, as if he had undergone a caesarean and something significant like his soul had been extracted. That lost thing was somewhere in the middle of the heaped coal. Anton began to rake through the heaped coal furiously with his bare hands. He grabbed large chunks of it and tossed them aside. The sharp edges cut his hands and blood ran over his skin. He paid it no heed and cleaned the road. However much coal he cast aside, the coal heap did not decrease. Holding up a larger chunk, he tossed it to the right and out of the corner of his eye saw how the coal disintegrated into dust. The strong wind grasped the cloud it had become and bore it somewhere behind him. He was startled and slowly turned around. A black wall hung in the air behind him. The wind was sweeping up the coal dust into buoyant currents, as if some unseen thing blocked the road behind him. An invisible barrier, and the black wall of coal dust now hung in the air there. Anton froze. The sight held him in its spell. The dust drifted in the air and black specks jostled one another. The whole structure rose from the earth and stretched into the depths of the sky. Even the clouds collided against that wall with their muzzles and, like vast agitated creatures, rumbled with dissatisfaction and trampled on the spot.

Anton's mouth gaped in astonishment. The wall of coal dust bustled like a living thing. Suddenly, it hung motionless. He heard a buzzing, the rustling of billions of particles of that dust wall as it began moving again. Anton whistled in amazements, still fascinated by this spectacle. After half a minute he understood that the wall was moving towards him, but it did not seem menacing, even though it accelerated. Perturbed and frightened, Anton stepped backwards slowly; he stumbled over a piece of coal that rolled under his feet, his body hit the ground painfully and his head collided with another lump of coal. Pain sheared his skull in half, but it was too late to think about his agony. That vast blackness oscillated, the wall approached and was now half a metre from him.

"No, anything but that," screamed Anton, as he woke and jumped off the cutter. He was in the mine with darkness all around. His miner's lamp made a sliver of the workings visible from the murk. There was no one nearby. Breathing irregularly he leaned against the conveyor belt. The river of coal flowed into the distributor. The monotonous drone of the engine soothed him and the images of his dream slowly faded into his consciousness.

Anton did not sleep again before the end of his shift. When he returned home, the first thing he wanted to do was to get close to Liuba, who was due to give birth soon. He entered the apartment and the bedroom where things were strewn untidily. The bed was still made and empty. Anton took off his clothes and pulled on the pants he wore around the house. He pulled out the wet towel he had dried himself with in the mine's changing room and hung it on the radiator. The soap on the windowsill had dried out.

Liuba was sitting in the kitchen smoking and Anton silently approached her and leaned against her belly. He heard the beating of a heart in her womb, which sounded as though it had come from the other side of the universe. The sound was still strange to him, but also close and familial. He had never experienced such a sensation of infinite kinship and stayed like that for a minute. Liuba, stunned, looked at her half-naked husband squatting on his haunches and listening to the tranquillity that rested in her womb. Neither spoke and silence wove itself around them. They were like two, no three, people united in the same locked circle. And no one on the planet wanted to cleave apart this unity. The usually morose Liuba smiled unexpectedly.

Chapter Four

Separatists have seized the provincial council premises in Luhansk. They smashed windows on the first floor and broke into the building. Subsequently, the Luhansk police left the province administration and council building and went to the military facility to surrender their weapons. Earlier, one of the police officers exited the province administration building and approached the separatists. He introduced himself as Colonel Sergei Osipov and announced that his unit was in the building to preserve order. He also told the separatists that he had led his 'blood-smeared and scorched fighters' from the Maidan in Kyiv. After negotiations with the separatists occupying the building he partially agreed to their demands. The separatists offered no compromises and insisted the police hand over their weapons, which would be sealed away.

The NBN site, 26.04.2014

One week later Anton got very drunk. According to mining tradition, a novice presents his colleagues with a three-litre bottle of samohonka on their first proper working day. After a shift the miners usually take the lift to the surface and go to the nearest tree plantation to drink, unless it is winter. They leave their packed lunches on the surface because they need a bite to eat when drinking.

Before starting work Anton went into the changing room where the mining master assigned him to his temporary working role. The mining master also made him sign the journal containing the safety regulations. Anton had barely entered his cubicle when Kostia darted towards him. Kostia, a thirty year old man with a guttural voice, asked, "Well Anton, did you bring anything?" He winked and smiled.

"Well, I'm going *you know where* when I resurface," replied Anton.

Ten minutes later the miners dashed hurriedly to their first job, having a cigarette. A few dozen men stood by the entrance to the plant and their coiled smoke rose skywards. Anton was not a smoker but he kept his friends company, standing with them and listening to their chatter. He had worked at the mine for almost one month, but he could not get used to the swearing the miners used while conversing. His father, although he drank, never swore around his children. Anton was a bit uncomfortable, but the last thing he wanted was to show that he was different, so he joined the conversation, cursing the 'Oranges' and abusing Yushchenko. Without perceiving the transition, he had crossed some imperceptible line and left his old self behind. He worked out this had happened on that very same day.

The shift, unfortunately, was particularly hard. He was put to work alongside three other men, rather than on the distributor. They had to lug an old pump engine from some redundant mine workings. Anton's companions were Kostia and an older man, who was about fifty and whose name he did not know. The older man groaned as they ascended the slope. Kostia chuntered incessantly about his years in the army; Anton was silent, as if trying to capture, memorise and imprint himself with that moment. He probably had a presentiment that he had passed the point of no return.

In order to pull the engine to its destination, they had to pass along eight hundred metres of a steeply angled section of the old workings. Then they needed to head right to emerge on to a gallery in a horizontal section of the mine. They traversed one kilometre, half of which lacked any rail tracks; in addition, there was a defunct area where the arched supports were dismantled and pieces of rock hung menacingly overhead; this was often the case.

The total length of a mine's workings can reach one hundred kilometres or so. When the coal in a section is exhausted almost all the equipment is removed, but sometimes equipment is forgotten in the rush to strip the area; as was the case now. The team were working their way towards their destination and were getting a little closer.

"Guys, look up carefully so you don't catch your head on the bare rock."

"Don't worry, Dad, I've already seen something like that – if you only saw my wife, after that even the devil isn't scary," muttered Kostia, and stepped confidently into the darkness.

For a few hundred metres ahead the section resembled a natural cave. The jagged walls of the gallery seemed as if they had been chewed out of rock. Sharply edged, many-hundred kilogram chunks hung down like pigs' carcasses in a butcher's freezer. Rotten boards were strewn underneath them, some whitish moss hung from the roof and large, dark puddles lay across the path.

"Come with me brothers," Kostia announced and glanced cautiously at the dangerous, overhanging rocks. The older man followed him, with Anton at the rear of the procession. They were knee deep in water and trampled mud, and jumped upon any little island of dryness whenever possible. The trio moved further into the depths of the earth. After twenty minutes a rift, about one metre high, appeared to the right in the gallery. This was a crosscut, a small working of about ten to twenty metres in length, running perpendicular to the other working. The other working was a breakthrough, similar to the crosscut, but much longer.

"Well, we've not gained much here, we've sweated buckets and will lose our minds dragging this thing," said the old man, taking off his helmet and scratching his head.

Kostia approached the crosscut and illuminated the murk with his lamp. There were props holding up the section of mine, but occasionally empty spaces gaped in the roof. "Sod it, we'll take the engine through the breakthrough, there are no winches, there's bugger all, we'll have to drag it," he said angrily.

"Let me check it," the old man said, clambering on to the aperture into the crosscut and illuminating it with his lamp. Then, irritably, he turned to Anton. "Go on Sonny, crawl in there, see how far it is."

Anton crawled into the crosscut. The engine was not far away so they decided to locate a piece of rope and drag it. After a minute Kostia squeezed into the crosscut. He simultaneously cursed the director, the president and the grandma who lived on the third passageway and would not give him any samohonka on the slate.

The engine, which weighed seventy kilograms, lay at the intersection of the crosscut and the working from where they were coming from the breakthrough. Two of them were needed to haul it. The rope was fastened to the engine and Kostia pulled while Anton pushed from behind. It was all going like clockwork, but they needed to exit the crosscut in a place where there were no props. The roof was bare with thin strata of rock, like layered cake, protruding.

"Come on, it's sticking, give it some," Kostia urged Anton as he tugged the rope over his back to the exit. He hit a prop, which fell, and plates of rock poured out of the ceiling. A dust cloud rose and a piece of rock weighing about ten kilos plummeted; its sharp end pierced Kostia's hand.

"Motherfucker," he yelled, almost instantaneously. His hand was pierced to the bone and blood poured over his boiler suit.

Anton rushed to help him. When he reached Kostia the wounded miner was moaning, while he looked in disbelief at the wound. Blood poured like water from a tap through the hole where the bone was visible. Anton's gaze was riveted to those red streams, his body reacted immediately and his bile rose. He had never seen so much blood.

The other miner, who Anton had characterised as an old

groaner, reached them. "Bloody hell, how are you?" He too was confused for a moment but he continued, "Anton, tear your shirt, we need to tie off the wound."

Anton did not react. He looked at the red stream spreading over the fabric like life fleeing that torn body. The wound was life turned inside out, existence flipped over, a mystery, the unravelling of torn flesh.

"Rip it, you twat, what are you waiting for?" the other miner urged.

Anton pulled off his shirt and with trembling hands ripped off its two sleeves. "Give 'em here." The old man ripped the sleeves from Anton's hands and bound Kostia's wound himself, muttering angrily, "They're employing boys who are still wet behind the ears."

Kostia emitted a muffled groan; Anton pressed his back against a prop and could not recover himself. During the rest of the shift he and the old man hauled the engine, which they had tied to a panel to make it easier to slide. They rested at fifteen minute intervals. Kostia lagged behind and red spots appeared through the sodden fabric binding his wound. Anton approached a couple of times to ask how he was, but Kostia remained silent, just nodding to show that everything was okay.

Weary, weak and exhausted, Anton was in a sombre mood as he emerged from the mine. It seemed to him that he had matured by several years in just a few hours. The men discussed the injury in the lift, but did not even consider cancelling the drinks planned for after work. On the contrary, they said it was needed more now to relieve stress and for its antibacterial effect. Kostia was sent to the infirmary and the rest set off to have a drink.

On the surface, after they had showered, the miners stood in a circle in a nearby tree plantation, with the three-litre bottle of *samohonka* in their midst. The appetisers were not bad, they ate salo, cucumbers, onions, and fried potatoes. The old man, who had helped Anton drag the engine, loudly told everyone how Kostia had got injured.

"So lad, let's drink to you now, you really understand that life is like a glass of vodka, one swipe and it's smashed," he said, smiling and proffering a full glass to Anton.

"Guys, I wasn't afraid really," Anton said, trying to justify himself, but no one was listening.

The knees-up swiftly became as garrulous as a market place. The hungry, tired miners got drunk almost immediately and their conversations became louder. A fight broke out. Anton became bleary and squatted on his haunches; he was tired of eating hard-boiled eggs, his head became clouded and the images of all around blurred imperceptibly. The miners chatted ever more noisily as Anton's temples hammered with memories of the shift, but the image of the accident gradually misted over. The other miners poured more alcohol into him. He drank, his legs began to give way and his conscious slowly fogged. The last thing he remembered was the old groaner yelling into his face that he had become a man.

The miners carried him back to the block where he lived, but Anton was unable to climb the stairs and had to sleep on the bench in front of the entrance. In the morning he stumbled up to his ninth floor apartment. *They really did need to move.* He was limited in his choice of location because a typical worker's salary then was two to three thousand hyrvnya.

The apartment Anton rented was expensive, so he also rented a private suburban house, long in need of renovation, for a few kopecks; he and Liuba planned to move there eventually. He needed to sort out his work too because they could not feed a third mouth in the family on the kind of income he received.

Two months later Anton transferred from stope mining to working at the 'long face wall or bench'. This was a horizontal mine working of between one and one and a half metres in height. Here, coal was extracted and transported to a linked sifting mechanism, similar to an iron trough. There were dozens of them interconnected by a continuous, narrow, iron strip on which a chain conveyor with wooden beams caught the newly mined coal. A combine, a longitudinal rectangular machine with cutters protruding from its body, moved the largest belt. The cutters were rotating, domed devices with crown-shaped cutting mechanisms at the end. These penetrated the dark and rocky mass and slithered along the conveyor to bring the fossil coal to the surface. It was a complicated task. The men manually pulled the machines, weighing one hundred to three hundred kilograms, or lugged sawn pine trunks of one and a half to two metres in length, or sifted through tons of rock and coal with a shovel. Here the ventilation was much worse than in the other mine workings and sometimes the air streamed out of the area.

The first time Anton descended into the mine it seemed like a submarine venturing into the depths. The feeling was incomparable. When he crossed the line of 'surface mine workings' he felt as if he developed an internal switch in his head. His inner state changed as if with a single click. The first stage was the struggle with darkness, which always occurred when Anton was sent into the depths of the old workings; he was always worried that the lamp might be extinguished. *And what would he do then? How would he get out if the people nearest to him were working five kilometres away?* The suspense was mingled with the fear of drowning in the darkness. The mine was filled with darkness and that fear now. Anton had to get a grip of himself and calm down. Even years later this troubling feeling remained somewhere in the depths of his soul.

The second impetus affecting that unseen switch was the fear of being different from the other miners; of being a white crow amongst them. So Anton tried to do everything he could so no one had occasion to accuse him of being 'apart from the collective'. He shared a few drinks with them after work and then carried his friends home; he worked until he was exhausted and swore incessantly. He thought and lived as a miner. This transformation occurred imperceptibly to, and perhaps even in spite of, himself because he never abandoned his desire to become an artist.

Anton eventually acclimatised to the hellish conditions of his job. The temperature in the stope reached forty degrees celsius. If he descended the mine shaft with two litre bottles of frozen water they would have completely melted when he reached the coalface. The heat often made the miners' noses bleed and they occasionally fainted.

"When we get to hell it will be like clocking on for a shift," the black-faced subterranean workers joked as they ate their packed lunches.

Miners often develop silicosis by the time they are forty. The coal dust mingles with the damp inside their lungs, hardens like a cobblestone and grows. There have been instances when a petrified lung had been removed from a miner, but they died in agony. And cases where, when the incision was made, the surgeon's scalpel had struck against the lung as if it were a stone. And how many deaths have there been in the mine itself? Death was as cruel as in the most fearful horror movies. Sometimes someone was caught in the rotators on the conveyor belt and all their innards, guts and skin were pulled off; it took a long time to remove their remains from the working. Miners remember such episodes all their life and recollect their lost companions as they down their bottles of spirits.

Once Anton was traversing a waterlogged section of the mine. His boots splashed through the water and gunk sprayed his hands. He was supposed to be going to a remote working where the men secreted their equipment. Miners quite often steal their kit from one another as well as their boiler suits and gum boots; that is why, when they are on the surface showering, dirty and clean clothes are locked away. The keys to their lockers are then buried in the mine, on the bottom or in the sides of the workings.

As he passed through the tunnel, Anton saw a light ahead of him and someone seemed to nod their head repeatedly. This happens sometimes because in the darkness the sole way to communicate with someone is to nod your head with the mining lamp switched on. Two nods mean 'pull, turn on the winch', a sideways nod means 'turn it off'. A circular nod means 'come to me'. It was a circular nod now.

"What, is he drunk? He's wagging his head like an epileptic," Anton grumbled. He occasionally talked to himself when he was alone and the shift seemed to stretch on endlessly.

Just a few seconds later he understood the reason behind the actions. The miner was suffering an electric shock. The mine wagons that carry wood are pulled by electric locomotives and resemble a tram. In the middle of the vehicles are poles which carry a charge from the power cables above them. The cables are suspended on brackets, stretched horizontally above the workings and are two metres above the floor. The charge in them is quite strong, upwards of 250 VDC. It is enough to kill someone.

The poor miner had got caught on the contact pole and was now jiggling about like a drunken teenager at a disco. A little more of this and his heart would give way. At best, random muscle spasms would cause fractures; at worst, they would throttle him. The man dangled like a rag doll and made a mindless bleating sound.

"Hang on, I'll be quick; just hang on a bit more," yelled Anton, and hit the man on the chest with a wooden board. In miner's jargon they call this a 'beat off'. A strong blow delivered to a man would allow them to break away from the electric charge holding them in its arc. The man's cotton boiler suit boomed with a sound like firecrackers. He flew one metre and bounced into a large puddle in the centre of the workings. His fall was imprinted in Anton's mind like a slow motion film; the grey body flying backwards into the water, the muddy puddle exploding, the helmet flying off with the lamp and being cast backwards and blinding him … the deafening moans of the victim, which seem to dilate time. In fact it all happened quickly, just a boom and the man was 'beaten off'.

"How are you? Alive?" Anton stretched his hand out to the other man.

The victim gasped, nodded, straightened his helmet and sat up. They were both silent for a couple of minutes. One froze, sitting on a plank, the light from his lamp flickering slightly, the other hung over him like a tree in the Donbas Steppe.

"What's your name, pal?"

"Nikolai Nikolaev," the other answered sheepishly.

Anton searched for some words he could use; he sorted through them as if by hand and tried to find a decent joke, but nothing came to mind.

"Well, that was bit clueless of you Nikolai Nikolaev. Can you move?"

"With difficulty," said Nikolaev, looking around as if searching for someone. But darkness covered the workings further away from them, nothing was visible there. There was just the one man he did not know trying to help him.

"What do they call you, pal?" Nikolaev asked hoarsely.

"I'm Anton. I suffered for that name in childhood because of that old cartoon, *Antoshka let's go dig spuds!* They used to sing that bloody song at me. Ever since then I've hated potatoes," Anton said.

Nikolai chuckled and then slowly, drawing out every word, he said, "I'll never forget what you did Anton."

Both miners squatted on one of the lengths of wood used in the mine. The silence tried to dissolve them within itself, but drops fell from the 'lock' on the fire prevention pipe and splashed on a piece of metal, methodically breaking this proverbial silence.

"Are you married?" Anton asked, for the sake of sustaining some conversation.

"Yes, I'm married. And I've got a lot on my plate. My mum's sick and bedridden, my dad's barely able to walk, he's eighty years old. My parents were long in the tooth when I was born. I guess you are married and live well?"

Anton hesitated momentarily because his marriage with Liuba had acquired its first cracks, so he said nothing about it directly. "My baby is due soon," he boasted, "I'm waiting for that moment. You know kids are a continuation of ourselves. I want to live in my daughter or son and for them to continue my existence."

"Hey brother, you've exaggerated what kids can do," Nikolai answered, smiling. "The fact is kids are as natural as winter snow and how will winter renew you?"

Anton did not understand the metaphor because he was used to simple verbal forms of communication. His new friend noticed his embarrassment and changed the theme. "Help me get to the surface."

They battled through mud, coal dust, and water tipping from guttering for more than two hours; their arms were around each other the whole time. Throughout that time they bandied tales and discussed the threads and intricacies of life's confused tangle.

After their joint ordeal they met several times before descending or ascending into the mine. People usually crowded on the landing while waiting for the lift to descend for the next shift. Anton saw Nikolai a couple of times and swapped a few words with him. Once they had met at the entrance to the mine's surface plant; Anton was hurrying for the bus but, seeing his friend, hugged him happily. Looking at them from the side you might have thought they were brothers.

Anton searched for some sense of kinship among the miners

because he felt as if he had been cast on to a desert island. He was nagged daily by these thoughts as he approached the narrow rift on to the bench section of the mine and saw the darkness pierced by the beams from miners' lamps. These roaming lights seemed to him like the fate of people frantically rushing around, searching for themselves. When he returned home after a shift he locked himself in the cubbyhole and set up his canvas and paints. His head was full of the mingled silhouettes, half-shadows and dust-smeared faces of the mine. He froze for a few minutes, then, taking his brush, felt like a bird soaring above a broken froth of clouds. His sweeping strokes created a startling dark world on the canvas, in the midst of which was an old man. The old man, Shubin, was the hero of miners' tales and had gone missing in a mining accident in the fifties. Now, whenever there was a knocking or a rattling in the mine, the miners said, "That's Shubin passing by."

Anton's painting depicted a man with coarse hands and rigid features, frozen at the entrance to the mine workings. The light of his lamp picks out the rusted arch and grey boards strengthening the sides of the excavation. He peers into the distance, as if searching for a way out, but can see no further than the beam of his lamp. Another canvas depicted the bus parked by the mine. Miners are exiting the vehicle in dirty boiler suits with tired, indifferent faces. One of them is Nikolai Nikolaev, the man Anton had rescued in the mine. Nikolai, who had been on the threshold of death, has knowledge which is inaccessible to others. The rest of the miners file past. There is a five year old boy standing to one side with a ball in his hands, contemplating the men intensely. He seems to be observing his own future.

Anton had only recently begun painting in this style. His childhood works were full of colours, shades and semi tones. However, over time, he came to paint the world as he saw it now, dark and plain. His canvases resembled the late work of his father more than his own early creations.

Nevertheless, in spite of the emergence of new paintings, every attempt at entering the university was accompanied by some fiasco. *Why spend money on it?* He travelled to the exams in Luhansk with a heavy heart. When he returned home he felt a lead weight in his chest, a presentiment that nothing would come of it. Arguments flared up between Liuba and himself at each attempt. Then the smouldering conflict began to break out between them on any occasion and for no reason. Their relationship became fractured with hostility and misunderstanding. Liuba would often not talk to him.

When he had returned from the meeting with Petrovych, when they awaited the Banderites, he went silently to his room and only told his wife about it in the evening. Liuba, now round-faced with hefty thighs protruding from a gaudy housecoat, smoked while sitting on a worn, wooden stool. Anton filled the stove with coal and told her about his day.

"They're idiots who won't do anything," Liuba summarised his tale emphatically, while flicking the ash off her cigarette. Anton watched the ash fall on his wife's exposed thighs and thought for a moment about whether to quarrel with her or have sex.

Chapter Five

Rumours that five buses with armed Banderites have arrived at the mine's dynamite warehouse have swept Rovenky. The Banderites surrounded the area, allegedly loaded the explosive on to the buses and were now able to blow up the bridges in the town. Dozens of Rovenky's inhabitants went to the scene with the worthy intention of saving their relatives. However, on arriving at the scene from different areas of the town and meeting at the warehouse, they mistook each other for Right Sector extremists. A wall-to-wall brawl ensued with everyone beating up whomever they wanted. Luckily, after a while, the brawl stopped and they advanced to meet the Banderites. They stopped and searched cars and rummaged through them. One truck did not stop, despite the men brandishing clubs and waving their arms dementedly in the middle of the road. After a brief chase, they caught the truck, beat up the driver and smashed up the vehicle, damaging the truck. The police who attended were surprised to discover there were no Right Sector extremists. The driver was sedated and they needed to charge someone. But who? The 'Cavaliers', the defenders of the homeland wearing St. George's Ribbons, who staggered all around them.

From the Novoye Vremya site, 10.05.2014

Two weeks passed and the Ukrainian military did not enter the town. However, several dozen Cossacks from the Rostov-on-Don area of Russia secretly infiltrated Rovenky in early May. They were supposedly soldiers of the Vsevelikoe Voisko Donskoe, a paramilitary formation taking its name from the Don Cossack Republic of 1918 to 1920. They arrived late at night in an utterly unceremonious manner. There were no horses or carts as they entered under the dense covering of darkness. There were only a couple of *Zhiguli* cars and a shabby *Zil* limousine cruising along a country road. After a few days, the town was as feverish as a pair of local drunkards on pay day. Thirty or so people stood on the central square by the town hall near an alley of lush green chestnut trees. Old soviet songs blared out from massive speakers. The wind furled and unfurled the occupiers' flags fantastically. A thoroughly inebriated man held a new banner belonging to the 'Luhansk People's Republic'. The microphone passed from hand to hand and they all repeated variations of the same cry, "The fascists have come to power in Kyiv." They condemned the junta and the followers of the Euromaidan. They claimed that, *Donbas will hear us*, and asked why cabbages had become so expensive. The concentration of slogans in the minds of the town's inhabitants had reached its peak. It seemed that nothing and no one could surprise them now.

Then, shunting aside onlookers, a fifty year old with short, grey hair and a serious visage appeared. He strode decisively, like Lenin, towards an armoured car. The newcomer's face wore an expression that only usually appears when being interrogated by the police. The green camouflage jacket of a Cossack, which was cast over his shoulders, fluttered like a medieval knight's cloak. This image was worthy of capture by a local photographer. It could have been printed in the local papers with captions such as 'the mysterious coming' or 'he came from the people', but there was no photographer nearby. The stranger unhurriedly approached the microphone, turned to the crowd and placed his khaki-panted legs, military-fashion, slightly apart. He called for silence and held up his hand, but the crowd did not quieten. In response, the stranger looked menacing and probably even more enigmatic. His whole appearance instilled fear, but the sole indication of this 'superman's' mortal origin was his red sneakers with long, blue laces.

"It has commmmme tooooo passss," he announced, drawing out the words, "that I am the military commander of this city and all powers have been transferred to me."

The throng fell silent. The citizen with the banner lowered it slowly. Old ladies abruptly lowered shopping bags to the floor. They all tensed and waited for this, until now, unknown, commander to continue his speech. Only a local dog remained indifferent to the speech of the new arrival; he continued to scratch his fleas while sitting under the nearest chestnut tree and calmly watching the crowd.

The medically sterile silence was broken by the most daring woman present, who was wearing a blue beret, "What do they call you, dearie?"

The self-proclaimed head of all Rovenky drilled into her with a gaze like that of the renowned, but ageing, hypnotist Kashpirovsky and replied, "Call me Ilyich."

The inhabitants of Rovenky, weary of the news about the Maidan and general provincial tedium, welcomed the arrival of a military leader with passion. He, with his whole Cossack soul, raised the mood of the crowd as far as he could. He announced mobilisation. They would capture members of Right Sector. He presented them with the frightening prospect of Anglo-Saxon troops coming to Donbas, but deep inside the commander understood there were no Anglo-Saxon troops in Rovenky. *Why should the inhabitants of Rovenky and Anglo-Saxon troops battle each other? Where was the logic?* These were the things he pondered during the long tedious evenings in Rovenky.

Ilyich entertained himself there as best he could; he drank to the point of unconsciousness, groped women, threatened to march on Kyiv and *string 'em all up on poplars to bring order.* However, ultimately, Ilyich decided to enter the history books not on horseback, clean shaven and brandishing a sword, but like a fifty year old Cossack. That is, he would head straight for the annals of history, drunk and with a beer sodden moustache.

The word annals had its own meaning for Ilyich and his coarse tongued companions, however, he tried not to speak it out loud because he knew the Cossack brethren would laugh and say, *Our father has gone off the rails.* So instead he said simply, "I will enter history."

And he did enter history, albeit barely able to stand, like a typical Cossack. He pronounced a young couple, with a small child, man and wife, under the power vested in him by the fictitious country, the Luhansk People's Republic. Ilyich began to conduct wedding ceremonies and construct bridges between aching hearts. He oversaw the whole process with his sombre, genuine Cossack face, which resembled a drunk janitor's visage. He would have added 'voila' to conclude the ceremony, but such fancy words were unknown to him.

"Get yourself a man, woman," Ilyich would say, showing some middle-aged female a timid, swarthy man. And they would have a knees up and the cry of "cheers" would echo, plastic cups would foam with cheap 'champagne', and a rare smile would play on his face. He had, at least for a day, banished boredom.

The commander loved to repeat the phrase, "The sea will flow over our street," while downing a glass to the health of a young couple.

Anton learned of the town's new chieftain one week after the Cossacks had appeared in Rovenky. On that day he was returning home with Petrovych and decided to withdraw some cash from the ATM in the town centre. His neighbour was endlessly telling him the brazen lies broadcast by the Russian TV channel, *LifeNews. The Ukrainian military on the occupied territories had crucified a child and forced their mother to watch. Ukrainian volunteer battalions had cut out the hearts of captured Donbas citizens and devoured them to frighten the enemy.* Alas, Petrovych thought they were all true. He would not shut his mouth and, like a machine gun, sprayed Anton with successive portions of horror.

Anton treated the Russian propaganda with distrust.

Ukrainians were a single people, how could they crucify and eat each other? He looked thoughtfully at his feet. The strip of pavement, like smeared chocolate, lay unevenly alongside the road; between the paving slabs slim green stalks of grass broke through the concrete.

They met a crowd at the ATM who were buzzing like one of the mine's huge ventilation fans. "What's going on here?" Petrovych asked, accosting a young man in a shabby blue jacket.

"There's no cash and there isn't going to be any," the other replied, calmly turning and walking slowly into the distance. His blue jacket remained visible on the horizon for a long time.

Anton did not understand what had happened. Squeezing inside the bank, he peered into the throng. A familiar voice asked everyone, without success, to stop shouting. When he finally reached the centre of the crowd, Anton realised that the voice belonged to Mitia, his old mining buddy, who was sitting on a wooden stool near the ATM. He looked strange now; his face was clean shaven, his hair combed, his hands did not shake, and there was no sign of a hangover. That would usually only mean one thing; his body had already received a dose of alcohol and this was relaxing his muscles. His breathing would surely be circulating that familiar alcoholic vapour. His eyes would be wandering in search of a litre to wash down the last one. But now…

Anton drew closer, not believing his own eyes, and what he ultimately saw shocked him. Mitia was in brand new camouflage fatigues. His trousers were tucked into black combat boots and his belt was adorned with a holster, à la the 1920s. Anton would not have been as amazed if he had seen a *chupacabra*. No one had ever seen Mitia sober. This fact was often the subject of jokes in the mine. They said he was born drunk and his first action was to ask the midwives for a bite to eat and one hundred grammes of vodka to celebrate his arrival on the earth. The celebrations had in fact lasted throughout Mitia's life and up to the present day. Now the absolutely sober Mitia had held the attention of the crowd for ten minutes. He told them that the junta had already stopped funding Donbas; after several vans delivering cash were attacked and heists undertaken at Privatbank and Oschadbank, the Kyiv fascists had closed all the branches and ATMs. It was unclear how people would get paid now.

The stunned Anton looked at the smoothly shaven chops of Mitia. He quoted the words of Panikovskyi, a comic Soviet cinema character, *And who are you?* Amid the uproar and panicked cries no one questioned what entitled Mitia to tell them how to live. In response, the ex-collier stood up, climbed on a chair and straightened his holster. He slowly lowered the camouflage jacket and stood straight, as if on parade. Finally and pompously he said, "I am Ilyich's vice-representative."

"Which Ilyich? Vladimir Ilyich Lenin?" Anton, who was standing below Mitia, asked in genuine incomprehension.

In response Mitia looked down and continued by pronouncing the letters in the word *y-e-s* so clearly that the crowd became a little frightened. Then he spoke of the situation in the country, the pressure from the USA and the will of the people. At one point he thrust his hand in his pocket, Lenin fashion, and bellowed with all the power of his well-smoked lungs, "The commander has appointed me his vice-representative."

Such an uproar then emerged from the crowd that Anton was unable to hear the ex-alcoholic's speech until its conclusion. The only thing to compare with the phrase he had just heard was a well-known phrase from a soviet film, '*The Lord appointed me as his beloved wife'. Mitia? A wife? Madness. What was going on in the town?*

The incitement continued, the camouflage-wearing orator on the stool shouted about the beginning of a new era. Now the oligarchs and those cursed nazis in Kyiv would not control Rovenky. This city, which fed all Ukraine, would now live the lifestyle of a Saudi oil magnate.

"Comrades, comrades," Mitia began with his favourite phrase. But the usual *c'mon, let's get drunk,* did not follow. After all, the vice-representative had not drunk for three days, and neither his wife, nor late mother-in-law, nor the medic treating his addiction, had ever achieved that. Indeed, the medic himself had got so drunk after Mitia's third visit that he left his practice and the city. Few knew what had made Mitia so ill. There were a couple of rumours, but that is another story. After his customary salutation to the 'comrades' Mitia's speech eschewed any reference to a booze up.

"I've got my life back," announced the right hand of Ilyich. "Look how freely I breathe. The Kyiv government regarded us as scum and wanted to fence us in with barbed wire. They wanted to be rid of us. Money won't be a problem. Soon Russia will take us in and then we'll live well."

Yesterday's alcoholic seemed to hover above his compatriots. His hand rose like a rocket aimed at the sky. The people, quietened now, listened to the living evidence of a miraculous rebirth. A force unknown to them, an energy broke the bent back of Mitia and reset it, presenting them with a new man. His every gesture now was similar to the sweep of the wings of a bird which has suddenly regained its freedom and now soars through blue recesses among woollen clouds.

Chapter Six

The inhabitants of Rovenky participated in the 11 May referendum, which asked them whether they supported the independence of the Luhansk People's Republic. The city's electoral commission reports that all the polling stations were opened at 08.00hrs. According to their data, over 48,000 of the city's inhabitants, almost 76% of the eligible voters, participated in the referendum; 98% of them said, 'Yes' in response to the question of whether they supported the independence of the Luhansk People's Republic.

From the Rovenkovskie Vesti newspaper, 12.05.2014

The day after the uproar at the bank, Anton decided to accompany his wife to the market. You need to have lived in the Ukrainian provinces for at least ten years to understand this, almost religious, ritual. The trip on Saturday or Sunday to the central square in town, where dozens of old women drag string bags as long as Gandalf's beard, young couples stroll, as if in a park, between the lines of stalls, girls measure camisoles against their sweaters, someone stands in their underpants, for all to see, to try on a pair of jeans, and an old man with a wheeler basket, who has bought a kilogram of potatoes, stands with his medals jingling in front of the collective farm workers selling cheese and sour cream from their stalls.

These allurements of life on the market are inaccessible to the inhabitants of large cities with shopping malls and boutiques. The cult of the market in provincial towns is so significant that for many locals the word boutique is almost offensive. Inhabitants of large towns do not know what it is like to try cottage cheese in a small place like Rovenky. A ruddy-cheeked lady with a hefty bust stood with her bosom overshadowing the products. It was no wonder that a huge queue of men formed by these stall. Sampling the dairy products successfully can be a substitute for watching a porn movie at the local Komsomolets cinema.

Anton worked his way down the queue for meat and bought a kilogram of pork tenderloin and a round of blood sausages. Then he decided to go to the collective farm stalls. People from nearby villages were selling fruit and vegetables there. The market was usually open until eleven or twelve o'clock and the collective farmers usually arrived at about four or five o'clock in the morning.

As he walked his usual route, Anton did not see the peasants he was familiar with, although it was still early. Instead, a trio in camouflage fatigues strolled ahead of him, two of whom had Kalashnikovs slung over their shoulders. A skinny, attractive woman, bottle-blonde with black roots, strutted in front of the armed escort. As she passed the stalls she pointed at the price tags and said something.

Recent events had taught Anton to be prepared for anything; he would not have been surprised if the woman's skull had opened and a tiny alien crawled out. As he drew closer, he heard her argument with one of the stall holders.

"Oksana, those would be the prices anywhere," the stall holder, a man with large, calloused hands looked imploringly at the woman.

"I said drop them - and that means drop them," she responded, tapping a red-varnished nail on the ripe tomatoes. "They are conducting bourgeois demagogy here. With prices above the stipulated ceiling, how will people live?"

It became clear that the market was now administered by the military. Only two members of its former leadership remained, an accountant and an engineer; just the technical personnel. The military administration now conducted a daily sweep of the market. They examined the prices and warned all the 'violators' that a second infringement would be penalised. The head of the hulk with the tomatoes was practically spinning.

Oksana, instead of wasting words, pulled out a piece of paper printed with the words: *Recently, the administration of the market has noticed that Rovenky's inhabitants are dissatisfied with the high prices. From 1 June, anyone who raises their prices or cheats the town's inhabitants will be fined by the militia.*

The paper fluttered and Oksana sighed like a city girl at a village disco surrounded by clueless bumpkins in big, tarpaulin-legged boots. The stall holder was humbled and, placidly taking a pen, reduced the prices by one-third. The scene with the manual control of prices would have scared any economics professor, but the reduction of prices by the sweep of a militia woman's hand did not perturb any of the customers. The soviet stereotype that everyone who trades is a speculator and a financial scammer who did not earn an honest living, still thrived here. Some of Rovenky's citizens even stopped near the camouflage-wearing trio and raucously praised their work.

The spirit of the soviet era hovered bird-like over the town and many of the local settlements. Occasionally, it seemed as if the USSR had not collapsed. Indeed, the Soviet Union had just thickened in East Ukraine, as fog gathers in fissures where fresh air does not reach. The area's inhabitants dressed fashionably and learned the words 'barter', 'WiFi' and 'boutique', but little of their interior nature had changed. Old soviet songs and chanson rang out of new mobile phones. Those who desired could parade through the town, though it would degenerate into a collective group stagger in this new era. Despite all this, none of it made the soviet-style people of Donbas more independent. That internal Homo Sovieticus remained alive in some and ready to do battle with the fascists. They blamed the flaws of the US State Department as blindly as they trusted the word of their leaders, like Ilyich, who had appeared out of nowhere and whom they feared and despised.

When, one week later, a rumour swept the town that the commander had caught a drunken taxi driver and ordered him to be flogged in the main square, no one was surprised. The celebratory flogging was scheduled for the weekend. Petrovych, as was now tradition, dragged Anton from his home. They would see how the new administration managed the town. A few hundred people gathered in the square.

At noon exactly, Ilyich, wearing his camouflage fatigues, firmly strode in position before the bored throng. The trussed and hapless taxi driver was led behind him with a heavily crinkled carrier bag from the ATB supermarket over his head. A rumble of astonishment echoed through the crowd. The inhabitants of Rovenky had not seen such medieval pageantry since the visit of a Mongolian Circus in 1977. Their visit had ended tragically when a strongman was gored by a bull he had literally failed to grab by the horns.

The crowd froze in anticipation as the victim was led to the central square. The terrified taxi driver remembered every deity out loud and his grandmothers on his father's and his mother's sides. He reached as far back as Adam and Eve. Just as they were misled by the devil, so the evil one had appeared to him as his friend Vasia with a bottle of vodka. Ilyich was as calm as a boa constrictor devouring a rabbit and as he bent to re-tie his blue shoelaces he waved his hand, condemning his victim. A Cossack in an appropriate shaggy fur cap approached the taxi driver. The crowd froze. The Cossack slowly circled the hapless driver, who had been laid horizontally on three chairs, as if choosing where to start. Tension crackled in the air. The executioner lingered, swatting the flail against his hand. An old woman in the front row nervously tapped her walking stick against the tarmac. Suddenly, the Cossack whipped the taxi driver with all his force, leaping into the air. The crowd moaned and the old lady, startled, waved her walking stick in front of herself like a gun. The next second, when the victim cried with pain, the crowd stepped back. The Cossack waved his whip in the air a few times and the old lady stunned Ilyich by bellowing out, "The Mongolian show was nothing at the side of this."

The commandant fussed with his hair until the end of this public torture, while ruminating painfully about what the Mongols had to do with it. The Rovenky dwellers were so enthusiastic about the beating that they ignored the old woman's words. Then the Cossack whipped the taxi driver so viciously that the lash whistled in the air. The thudding of the blows echoed between the walls of the residential blocks around the square. The taxi driver contorted with his cries and the crowd stomped a little in time with the blows. Only Ilyich frowned somewhat, looking around himself and despairingly seeking the reason for the old woman's Mongolian comment.

The punishment ended and the Cossack rolled up his whip. The taxi driver rose from the chairs, groaning, and silence covered the square. But the commander still pondered in the depths of his consciousness, *What did the Mongol have to do with it?* Half a minute later his mood changed. The shadow fell from his face and he forgot about the taxi driver and the representative of the Mongolian race. Now another matter concerned him. He pulled a twisted piece of paper from his pocket, smoothed it out and read aloud an announcement to the throng on the square. They were recruiting locals into a new militia.

"Donbas is working class," Ilyich declaimed. "While we laboured here, they staged a revolution in Kyiv and now they are gathering troops to send here and quell us. These monsters have slaughtered whole villages. Not long ago, in Novosvitlivka, they seized a collective farm representative, hung him on the square and burned the womenfolk alive in a barn. Do you want that here?" He waved the paper. He proclaimed that those who wanted to defend their country should join up. The frivolities were over. This was war.

The words agitated the crowd at least as much as the public flogging. Anton listened to the commander in disbelief.

Yes, he had seen the news from Kyiv: the burning tyres, the Maidan, the wounded Berkut fighters. The media kaleidoscope had presented him with utterly new images. Even his sporadic exchanges with his older brother, Sergei, who had lived in Kyiv, but moved to Munich at the end of last summer, failed to soothe him. *But why should he wage war? Why should he, a miner who yearned to become an artist, be compelled to take up arms?*

Anton saw the handsome priest, Father Vladimir, in the crowd. The silver-haired old man served in a small church in the Chernigovskii residential area and Anton had first attended one of his services a year ago. Anton was hopelessly addicted to slot machines at that time. The arcades where he gambled were officially closed down but there were a few secret premises where three or four of the machines operated. He would often sit late at night in a cramped, dark room, usually the basement of a residential block. He frittered away one-third of his salary. Once he was once lucky enough to win two thousand hyrvnya. A symphony orchestra played in his heart and the world seemed brightly painted. In his delight he continued to play and lost and lost again, until he had lost thousands more than he had won.

Anton decided to put a stop to his addiction. Liuba took charge of his money and bent his ear, but clearly not enough. After one such conversation Anton squandered half of his available money. He then turned to Christ in his next attempt to banish the slot machine demon and went to the local Orthodox church where he saw Father Vladimir. He crossed himself ineptly at the entrance to the building. Anton had admittedly never fled God, but he also had not approached the deity. He also had no interest in going to the homes of Christians and socialising with them. He asked himself if he was sinful and concluded that the answer was yes.

The stately, sinewy Father Vladimir, so unlike the average priest, spoke plainly with Anton without trying to convince him of anything. "You understand that, broadly speaking, God is external to existence and man sees everything that exists in the world as an observer. And here a question arises: which came first, the observer or the world? It's the 'chicken and egg' question. If the observer came first, where could he exist apart from the world. This means the world came first. However, if the world came first, who recognised it as the world? The observer, obviously, is the winner here. So we have a paradox. It becomes clear that there is a third party, who is external to both these elements. That is God. God is above everything. So he will help you."

Father Vladimir's speech spoke of things that were new to Anton and he visited the priest a few more times. They sat in Father Vladimir's gazebo, the wood of which was swathed in flowers, which seemed to embrace the structure like a lover. A huge green bush loomed nearby, like a wave that might at any moment overwhelm the fragile timber edifice. It reared over the gazebo as if about to fall, but was frozen suddenly in mid surge and cast a huge shadow.

"Someone said that the pleasure of life lies in the absence of pain," the priest gently lectured Anton. "Start small, solve your immediate problems and these decisions will give your life meaning."

Anton once arrived at the priest's place drunk and simply wanting to talk to someone. The clergyman did not drive him away. He listened for a long time as Anton abused Liuba, expounded his desire to achieve greatness, and described his paintings. Anton talked about the images gathering in his head and how he should liberate them, for they were real people. They entered this world, but the world did not accept them.

"How can I bear this, Father?" Anton asked in anguish. "My soul is like a cask in which wine ferments. It has long matured and if not decanted it will turn to vinegar," he said, forcefully smacking his fists together.

"Who shows you these images, my son?" the priest asked in reply. "If there is no way they can emerge it means they are not given to you by God. They are, therefore, from the devil. Be humble, do not be proud of your own deep spirit. There is much that is superfluous within you there."

Anton was briefly silent and then spoke further. He described his lack of vitality, and how Liuba tormented him, drinking his life blood and not allowing him to be himself. He endured all this because of his family, but was considering divorce.

Father Vladimir groomed his beard without hurrying to reply. He strode to and fro across the room and stared intently at Anton. "Divorce is a terrible sin. Look at the scripture. Jesus said he who divorces commits adultery."

On that day Anton left the priest with a sense of some imminent doom, the circle around him was tightening daily. He felt as if something were strangling his life force in the vicinity of his heart. It crushed him and prevented him from basking in his secret inner world. Only his painting could renew his sway over himself. He could not weep and release his frustration. There were times when no one was at home and he stood before the icon and bowed. He envisaged his words reaching heaven and wiped away his rare masculine tears at his hopeless plight. He visited the priest a couple more times after he had finished work. He confessed and received communion. He repented and searched for some light in the darkness; whether he would find one he did not know; but he gave up playing the machines.

Now, listening to Ilyich's speech about war and recruitment to the militia, Anton, in bewilderment, decided to sound-out the priest's views. "Father, is waging war pleasing to the Lord."

"Yes son, defending the fatherland is a sacred cause," murmured Vladimir quietly.

On returning home, Anton cast off his boots and sat

on the stool in the hallway. Liuba had started sleeping at her mother's place and had taken the children with her after their last quarrel. Prior to leaving, she had come to the door of the room where he sat and practically hissed, *Waster,* at him. The word swirled around his world, along with the phrases *sacred cause and militia, divorce and sin.* All this verbal mixture churned in Anton's head like ingredients in a food processor. As if it were all being prepared to be tipped into a frying pan or a dustbin.

Chapter Seven

On 13 June, Mr. B, a resident of Rubizhne, born in 1961, was travelling in his red Lifan X 60 car. He encountered a checkpoint on the bridge over the Borova river in the city of Sievierodonetsk. An unknown group of masked men stopped him. They were armed with automatic weapons and wore camouflage fatigues with St. George's Ribbons. They stole his car at gunpoint. On 17 June, at 13.30, in the city of Zorinsk, by the Zorinskaya café on Leningradskaja Street, three unknown men, armed with automatic rifles, presented themselves as militia. They stole a white Volkswagon Transporter from a Mr. F, who was born in 1955. Another incident occurred on 7 June, at approximately 15.45, on the Kyiv-Khrakiv-Dolzhansky road, near the turning for Fashchevka village in the Antratsyt district. A group of people armed with automatic weapons, wearing camouflage fatigues and bearing the LPR flag, stopped a grey Seat Leon car driven by a Mr. B, born in 1971. They stole the car at gunpoint.

Press service of the Ukrainian Interior Ministry, 18.06.2014

Sergei Nedelkov was closing the door of his one-roomed apartment in a residential block on Munich's Metzstraße when his mobile-phone rang irritatingly with a text message. He had wanted to change the ringtone many times but was still hearing it. His patience was tested to the limit by this and he was now late for work at his office, which was five blocks away. He held a bag in one hand and an umbrella in the other because of the current spring showers. Sergei heard another ring tone and recollected that he had an old Nokia phone he always carried, despite never using it. His mother had given him this when he was still living in Rovenky and had successfully completed his first course at the IT faculty of Luhansk University.

Sergei's interest in computer programming had emerged

when he was still at school. In the evenings he went to a computer club and, with trembling hands, inserted a floppy disc into an old computer to write his first salutation to the world. This imbued him with the confidence that he could construct a life with a similar code to that he used for programming computers.

In the year he completed his first course, he also realised that his attempt at programming a life had failed. One day in summer he was sitting on a wooden bench in the children's park smoking menthol cigarettes with his friend, Sashko Lonskyj. They spat occasionally on the decking in front of them in an attempt to look cool. Pasha Skliarov soon appeared with two girls, Lena and Tania, and they all went to have a few beers. After a while the group drifted to Lonskyj's apartment. There was a litre bottle of vodka, cheese, sausages and a couple of apples on the table. They drank until late in the evening. Sergei was sitting next to Lena and, unnoticed, even by himself, began to caress her back gently. Until then he had never had a girlfriend because he never met women socially.

Seeing the uninhibitedness of their drinking companions, he acquired the courage to suggest that Lena went to the bedroom with him. She agreed and ten minutes later he was pressing his naked body against hers. Lena stripped willingly, lay on the floor and spread her legs as if she had made love hundreds of times before. Sergei entered her, pushing a little clumsily, like a malfunctioning piston. He was anxious and a tide of thoughts surged through him. Lena, lying beneath him, concentrated on his face while he frantically squeezed her small breasts with his free hand. He had become acclimatised to their coupling now and accelerated his movements. His head resounded with a thought at once desperate and happy. *I am finally a man.*

The party finished at midnight and they all departed. Sergei, still half-drunk, went home and immediately felt the need to pass water. When he lowered his trousers he saw that his genitals were covered in blood. A red blotch seeped down his underpants from a large wound on his penis. He nearly fainted, his head swam and his bile rose. He slipped off the toilet, luckily everyone in the house was asleep, and headed for the kitchen. He opened the window and put out his head; the fresh air revived him like iced water. He relaxed a little, but could not understand what had happened.

Sergei suffered with the wound, which stubbornly refused to heal, for a whole week before he visited a surgeon, who immediately referred him to the STI clinic. The institution was at the far end of the town and situated in an ancient, two-storey building surrounded by private houses. Lush shrubs flourished in front of the edifice and shrouded the windows on the first floor. There were a few benches in the grounds and, a little further away, a half-dilapidated building.

" Soooooooo," said the doctor, stretching out the word as she examined Sergei. Then she looked intensely at him, as if trying to find the cause of his illness in his face rather than his penis. Sergei looked younger than he was. His pale-blue eyes, his bulging spud of a nose, high forehead and sensitive lips were not those of an eighteen year old. He looked, at most, sixteen years old. A minute passed. "You had intercourse recently?" she asked, turning her attention to a sheet of paper and marking out the possibilities carefully with a pen.

Sergei underwent various tests and returned to the clinic one week later. The same doctor inspected the papers with the results of the tests, occasionally peering at the patient from under her glasses. Then she examined his genitals again.

" Syphi-ii-ilis," she said, drawing out the word before raising her head and looking into his pale-blue, frightened eyes.

Sergei's heart fluttered as frantically as a humming bird. His hands trembled a little, but he could not say anything. His head replayed the scene with a naked Lena and her indifferent face. This cannot be right, he thought, the doctor has clearly mistaken the wound for a sign of syphilis.

"You need to get to the hospital," she said, breaking Sergei's chain of thought.

The next day Sergei stood by the reception desk of the hospital with some packages, waiting to be told which ward his bed was in. He, with his rustling paper-wrapped parcels, ascended to the second floor where ward six was situated. There were five beds on the ward. A red-haired man was lain on one of them, reading a yellowed newspaper left by a former patient. A twenty-five year old man lay on the second bed, and a grey-haired old man on the third; it transpired that he was seventy-two. His case history was that he had been happily married for over forty years until one day when a neighbour, a statuesque spinster, asked for his help to sharpen a meat knife. He told his wife he would pop out for a minute, but did not return until evening was setting in. After he had helped the spinster with her knife she asked him for a hand with the wiring, then something else and something else. They gradually got closer to the bedroom where she pounced on him. The solitary woman, wild with passion, reactivated the old man's urges, which had been dormant for decades, and they had sex without, of course, using any condoms. Three weeks later syphilitic ulcers appeared. The old man's name was Ivan Nikiforovich.

"My old woman almost fainted when she heard what had happened and grabbed her chest and then a knife. When I was coming to the hospital she came behind me and warmed my backside with a frying pan," Nikiforovich told them on the evening Sergei arrived. "After that she forgave me," he concluded, smiling sombrely.

The first night in hospital was particularly difficult for Sergei. He was prescribed a course of penicillin every four hours for a period of twenty-one days. He went to the nursing station and was given an injection. The nurse sighed when she saw him, such a pity, he was so young. She asked more than once how he had managed to end up in this lamentable place. Sergei just waved the question away, as if to say, it's irrelevant. One week later Sergei even had to stand when he ate; his backside hurt and was covered in bruises.

There was nothing to do in the hospital other than play cards with the red-haired man with a drinker's face, an intelligent man who had been admitted the night before Sergei, and the old man. The old man dealt the cards and told them what men he knew in his village thought had happened to him. They believed he was in a hospital bed due to a heart attack, and had even asked where he was so they could visit.

"My wife disguised herself with a headscarf around her face. She had cried her eyes out, the shame hurt so much. She said this was because of me, an old idiot. She had not come to visit me before because she wanted to kill me and said that I was a disgrace to the whole world," Nikiforovich said, paraphrasing his wife's words. He moistened his finger and dealt the cards.

"How are you going to make peace with her?" Sergei asked.

The older man was silent as he looked at the smiling face of his fellow penicillin-injection sufferer and then spoke, "I won't do anything. She doesn't bear a grudge for long. She'll be narked for a little bit more, then it'll all be over. I'm as used to living with her as you are to breathing and seeing things."

Nikiforovich dealt, his face wore an expression of calm as he concentrated on the cards. Sergei turned his head and saw the sun-rays filtered through a dirty net curtain. It was as if the light were tangled in tropical petals and flowers as it laboriously penetrated through the fabric, from the window on to the bed and cracked like an egg, leaving a white spot there.

Sergei was discharged ahead of schedule. The wound healed and the doctor said his test results were encouraging. He left the clinic and reflected how his companion had shuffled the cards like people were shuffled, while saying you could get used to anything.

Sergei completed his course but was unable to find any other work so became a lecturer in IT at the local mining technical college. It happened by the same chance which he now thought controlled his life. He faced the chore of teaching inept students daily, and eagerly searched for some error in the programming code of his life.

Many years passed. He remembered distinctly how, leaving one class late in the evening, he had entered a dark street illuminated only by the light from the windows of a nine-storey block. The city, even in its central areas and on main roads, lacked lighting. He had pondered then how someone who had lived half a life in the provinces would not have seen their own shadow on the streets at night. The darkness here was total. The shadow certainly hid more than was apparent. A shadow can be a form of identification in this world if you wish it to be; and part of many people's self identification is ruled by a darkness, like that holding sway over the unlit streets of a provincial town.

Sergei undertook such contemplative strolls more and more often. During one particularly sombre autumn he walked along, scuffing aside the dry leaves strewn on the pavement. The wind was damp, almost wet. Sergei was frozen to the bone and yearned for his favourite green tea and to pick up a book and then sleep. As he crossed the square he heard someone's dry cough and thought it must be some tuberculosis victim who had fled a clinic and was sitting on the bench that was coming into view. He quickened his pace to pass as quickly as possible, but he heard a voice as he drew level with the patient. It was so clear and deep that he thought it must belong to a university professor.

"Young man, please could you give me a match or a lighter, I forgot mine and left it at home. I would be genuinely grateful."

Sergei had last heard the phrase 'genuinely grateful' when he had defended his diploma at the institute. One of the elderly Luhansk lecturers from the seventies, who wore a long dress with a frill at the neck, had dropped a pack of papers, from which some sheets spilled, while walking along the corridor. Sergei had hurried to help her and she had said she was 'genuinely grateful' and even nodded slightly.

As he approached the 'professor' Sergei saw an elderly man wearing a worn grey-green coat and an unfashionable hat. His ageing hands were squeezing a filterless cigarette. Sergei had not smoked for a month but still had a lighter in his pocket.

"Please take it," he said, stretching his lighter-clutching hand towards the stranger.

"Oh, thank you," the professor said enthusiastically. "I've decided to torture myself thus in my old age."

Sergei wanted to continue walking, but some unknown force kept him with the stranger. It became clear as he talked that the old man had graduated from the philology faculty at Volgograd over thirty years ago. He had met a girl from Rovenky on his last course at the university and had moved to the town without having a job. He had ended up at the mine, but words still fascinated him. He always carried a small volume of Dostoevsky, Nabokov, or another of the classics in his pocket.

"All around there's dirt, dust and the racket, and I descended down the pit and quoted Tsvetaeva to someone I knew. Imagine it! Swearing, cussing and verses," the old man uttered with rapture.

Sergei listened enthusiastically. This stranger talked about the essence of his days, their elusiveness and how quickly they passed. He said that recently he had read the definition of the word freedom: it was 'sobriety'. People drank and used drugs to immerse themselves in utter oblivion and shed those arduous obligations that bring us freedom.

"What is the chief and heaviest obligation which freedom imposes? Sight. So we drink to blind ourselves for a while. You asked if I am satisfied with the life I have lived? Life is a moment which cannot be reckoned. It falls from time's clock hand and cannot be fixed with its arrow. It cannot be entered into a multiplication table of days. Life is the space between minutes. Understand this, life cannot be observed, touched nor examined. Existence is an emptiness concealed between the crannies of eternity. So it is hard to observe the moment in which you live. You only observe it when you have lived through it, but then it is often too late," the old man said, as if imparting an instruction.

As Sergei returned home, the stranger's words profoundly affected him; as if his soul were bleeding out. Two weeks later he cast everything aside, bought the first available ticket from Luhansk to Kyiv and headed for the capital. He would seek a better realisation of the programme code of existence.

He spent the first night at the railway station, sleeping on a bench with the bag containing his computer for a pillow.

"Son, keep an eye on your stuff," said a female cleaner, patting him on the shoulder as she passed.

"The main thing is they don't steal me, though who'd have any use for me," he grumbled, relapsing into sleep.

His last phase seemed to be true. Everywhere he went there was no work, and the money he had would only last one week. He went for interviews from morning to evening and finally, by some miracle, found a job at *Chips* magazine.

Three years later he was working in a subsidiary of the German insurance company, *Allianz*. Then, last year, after the intervention of the Kyiv office, he was transferred to Munich as one of the company's most talented employees.

Now, as the mobile phone chimed with a text message, Sergei was rushing to work. Grumbling irritably, he put down the bag and grabbed the telephone. The text was from a

Ukrainian number:

Sergei, something terrible has happened. Your brother has disappeared for almost a month. Help us if you can, Liuba.

Sergei thoughtfully drifted his finger down the phone, reading the message a few times. *How could Anton have disappeared? Had someone murdered him? Taken him hostage? Had the war in Donbas reached Rovenky?*

He telephoned Liuba. It emerged that a few weeks ago Anton had returned home late from work. He had not replied when she asked him where he had been. The following morning, when the children got out of bed, Anton was not in the apartment. That was all. He had just gone, leaving emptiness; no news. His father, Anatolii, had checked all the car parks, the town's outskirts and all the yards. It was as if Anton had disintegrated into his component molecules. The children thought their father was away on some business.

"What can I do, where can I look?" Liuba asked in confusion.

Chapter Eight

The DPR and LPR have agreed to a truce until 30 June

The self-proclaimed Luhansk and Donetsk People's Republics have agreed to a truce with the Ukrainian military until 30 June. The truce was announced by Aleksandr Borodai, president of the DPR. The announcement resulted from a round of negotiations on the conflict, which were held in Donetsk. The negotiations were held on 23 June, with the participation of representatives from Ukraine, Russia, the OSCE, and also the DPR and LPR. A previous round of negotiations had also agreed to a truce, however, military conflict in the area did not cease. Borodai referred to President Poroshenko's willingness to extend the formal truce by seventy-two hours, according to official sources. According to Prime Minister Borodai, the militia were also willing to extend the truce.

From the RIA Novosti site, 27.06.2014

Sergei knew that everything was not well in his brother's family; to put it mildly. His brother suffered at the hands of his wife but endured the situation because of the children. *How could he help Anton now? Telephone their father? They had not talked for a long time.* His father viewed Sergei as practically involved in the Maidan. Sergei, along with other volunteers who gathered money for medication and rifles for the front, had sent money from Germany for the revolution.

His father had initially called him on *Skype* and berated him for not supporting his relatives. Then he threatened to come to Kyiv and 'slaughter all of them in turn, as the Ukes slaughter people in Donbas'. Sergei tried to tell him this was all unfounded rumours, Russian TV lied blatantly and Right Sector had only polled one percent in the elections. However, his father had not been too fond of Kyivans since the Orange

76

Revolution of 2005.

The remnants of that antipathy were fanned by local politicians in Donbas, who had held an anti-fascist rally, organised by the Party of the Regions, a year before the Maidan. His father could not explain the reasons for his hostility towards Kyivans, which almost choked him. However, it had grown slowly inside his psyche like a seed. One day they had a protracted quarrel.

"The Ukrainian military conduct themselves like the Third Reich," Anatolii said, literally foaming at the mouth. "Recently a neighbour told me about her sister, who lives in Shchastia. There they say the Ukes went through the apartments, dragging out by the hair those who voted in the independence referendum. They shot them in the passageways."

"Dad, it's a lie," Sergei replied. "Get this, it's the Kremlin working to divide us. Who in their right mind would act like the Third Reich here? And it's just the opposite. Journalists write that the 'militants' cut open the bellies of captured volunteers. The Chechens cut off their ears and the Novorossiya military shell residential buildings."

It was clear the conversation had reached a dead end and the son began to address his father more warmly than usual. In a minute he was sure that the rusty iron carapace on his father's heart would fall asunder and the fragments fly apart.

"Dad, do you remember that time we were out on a walk and I said you were important for me? Do you remember how, after I graduated, I told you I loved you? And how I massaged you when you injured your back? Can I have changed that much? Why don't you believe that I am telling the truth?" the son asked his somewhat confused father.

The image on the screen of the tablet twitched. Anatolii flushed, clearly longing to say something acerbic in reply. However, for a second, deep in his heart, his paternal feelings pierced him.

"Why can't you understand that we want to live without oligarchs who have drained us dry?" he said slowly. "It's that simple - we desire social justice."

"But how is that, Father?" yelled Sergei. "Where do the militants get their weapons from? The Grad rockets, artillery guns, T 72 tanks? Russian army weapons? You are ready to suffer for an idea, but it's not yours, it's a foreign ideal. Now Putin wants war to tear Ukraine to bits. That'll be easier for him, he'll be able to stay in power then. How long has Poroshenko been running the country and how long were the Party of the Regions? Who brought you to this? You'll just be cannon fodder."

"Maidan Fascist, you are not my son. Come back to town and I'll be the first to hand you over to the militia," his father yelled as he ended the call.

Sergei did not call him back. He had long understood that he was a lesser son than Anton. His father loved the younger boy and saw him as a reincarnation of himself. The same curly hair, the same eyes, the same fascination with painting.

One winter, during their childhood, the children had stayed at their grandmother's. They had gone sledging on cardboard boxes down snowy hillocks above a small river with the neighbouring children. The boys hurtled down the steep slope and into a snowdrift on the riverbank. Anton persuaded the other boys to move from their usual spot to another place where the hill was higher and the slope down to the river was steeper. Sergei tried to stop them, but Anton, driven by some sudden emotional impulse, insisted. Eight year old Sashka was the first boy to sledge down the new slope. Settling himself on his box, he hurtled downwards with a cry that became louder and wilder after the sledge stopped. The snowdrift by the river here concealed a fallen tree. Sashka, when he was braking as hard as he could with his left arm, hit the trunk with it and snapped the bone. Although it was Anton's fault as the initiator, his father, pitying the younger boy, gave Sergei a good thrashing.

From that time onwards Sergei noted that his father excused and cherished his favourite son. His mother tried to soften the rejection for her older boy, but how could he get his father to love him in his heart?

Sergei stood in front of the door to his German apartment and thought how, for the sake of his brother, he should change his attitude towards his father, but he could not find the strength to forgive Anatolii. He flicked through his telephone book and found Zbigniew Podolski's number. The Polish OSCE expert, who had worked in Donbas, was a good friend of Sergei. He could be useful now.

After half a minute Sergei got through to him and heard his friend's familiar voice. Zbigniew promised to help. The self-proclaimed LPR, which occupied almost all of Luhansk province, apart from a fragment in the north, had just formed a ministerial cabinet. Another republic had formed alongside them; the DPR. The two republics had agreed to unite into a single entity, Novorossiya. Sergei had heard about this when President Putin spoke for the first time about that part of Ukraine where separatists battled the Ukrainian army. If this had initially appeared to be a bluff, the Ukrainian army and volunteer battalions had now retreated; four thousand regular Russian troops and five hundred armoured vehicles had entered Ukraine from Russia. Zbigniew laid all this out for Sergei with a tremor in his voice. The official position of the OSCE did not accord with Sergei's unofficial data. Foreign experts had, for an extended period, 'not observed' the Russian military in Ukraine.

"Do you understand this is a sub-culture among Europeans, they may espouse general liberal ideas but they will shy away from a conflict with Russia. The Kremlin has a powerful lobby in Europe, starting with journalists and reaching up to members of the European Parliament. It's just a business paid for with blood. Europeans are only interested in their level of unemployment and the price of tomatoes. Do you understand?"

Zbigniew was really asking himself, more than he was asking Sergei, these questions. However, Sergei heard almost nothing of these words. He was an idealist of the European world. He had argued in one hundred conversations with his Ukrainian friends that European civilisation was a step in human evolution. It began with an understanding of human rights and concluded with Europe's historical mission. He could not change his view, even after hearing the words of his close friend.

Sergei was hopelessly late for work. He caught a taxi and asked the driver to take him around the city. He hoped to quell his anguish by seeing the well-kept streets, level roads, straight paths and chance Germans. The city's people talked, gestured and often smiled in a carefree way. They knew nothing of his missing brother, estranged father, and the far away mythical republic of Novorossiya.

Chapter Nine

Ukrainian army soldiers are forcing civilians to cooperate with them. Those who oppose such cooperation are intimidated by the National Guard, which threatens to kill their friends and relatives. The National Guard recently terrorised citizens in Herasimovka, thirty-eight kilometres north-east of Luhansk, according to a deserter from the Ukrainian Armed Forces who recounted details of their actions there. They arrested the family of a local man who refused to help them, and burned down their house and small holding. It is not known what happened to the arrested man and two of his children. This is not the first time that Ukrainian troops have forced people to work for them. In August this year the LPR's press secretary, Vladimir Inogorodskyj, told Life News that Ukrainian troops had forced the inhabitants of Novosvitlivka to dig pits. Those who disagreed were shot in front of their neighbours. When the digging was completed National Guard troops drove these peaceful civilians into the church and mined it.

Life News, 10.07.2014

Ilyich sat in the mayor's leather chair. Empty chairs, like ships moored in a marina, stood by a long, brown table in the office of the city's leader. The table itself was cluttered with a plate, dirty with the remains of food, a partially drunk glass of tea and several crumpled napkins. Ilyich tapped his finger on the edge of the table, as if attempting to play a melody. He wondered how to occupy himself, but only vulgar ideas entered his head. "Perhaps vulgar reflections are okay? Certainly, if vulgarity is evil, does not good occasionally emerge from evil?" the new master of the mayor's office asked himself aloud. He smiled at such a pleasant evaluation of his own impulses.

Tapping his knuckles in a rhythm that resembled a military march, he cast his feet in their faded red sneakers with blue laces on to the table. After the city had surrendered to his governing, which was more accurately plundering, his sensitive and impulsive soul was troubled. Barely a month had passed since his ceremonial coming to power. "Something must be done or I could waste away here," he muttered under his breath before exiting into the passageway.

Ilyich did not find tranquillity as he wandered the long, unpopulated corridors of the city executive. He tested the strength of the nearest doors, kicked an empty bucket, went to a window and smiled at a crow sitting on a tree. The crow did not appreciate the commander's smile and took off sharply. That amused him a little.

He had a special relationship with birds and had owned a parrot in his childhood; the bird was named Kesha, in honour of a renowned Soviet cartoon parrot. The five year old Ilyich decided to conduct an experiment with his pet. He took an ordinary thread, tore his notebook into strips, twisted the strips into cylinders and wove the thread through them. Then he wrapped his construction around Kesha's talons. It must be said that the parrot was placid and did not make a sound as the boy fettered it with this structure. It did not understand what it was being condemned to by this mysteriously smiling boy in short trousers. Little Ilyich held Kesha in one hand, while the other held an already lit match with which he set fire to the lowest strip of paper. It was blazing in seconds and the little boy released his bird with fire trailing in its wake. Kesha shrieked and circled the room rapidly before flying through the open window. Ilyich dashed after the bird. The parrot cried frantically, a fire in the form of a bird, a phoenix, and plunged rapidly into a lush green tree like a downed Messerschmitt plane. From that moment birds had never liked him. Even the crow had sensed something and been frightened.

His position in the town meant Ilyich could not amuse himself for very long by languishing in his recollections, so the commander decided to conduct an inspection of his domain. He called Mitia and sat alongside him in the mayoral car while they drove through the city. The commander and his deputy visited the shops, peered into kiosks and chatted with the inhabitants. As they passed along the street they saw a sign saying 'Dental Clinic'. The entrance was guarded by a militia man. It transpired that the clinic's owner had fled, but had left the equipment and the guard was preventing looting.

Ilyich's heart pounded rapidly at the sight of a dental clinic. "Mitia, let's go in, there's something I need to get."

The sterile cleanliness of the clinic enraptured the commander. As they passed through the rooms he sat in the dentist's chair, opened his mouth and waved his hand. "C'mon Mitia, sort out my teeth." They both laughed.

This was the first time Ilyich had felt so relaxed at the dentists; as a child he had almost fallen into hysterics whenever he had a dental appointment. He saw what he was looking for; a nozzle with a rubber bulb for collecting and spraying water to rinse a patient's mouth. When he was a child sitting in the dentist's chair, he yearned for the drilling to stop and the need to rinse his mouth was his only salvation to halt his suffering. The rinsing apparatus became a symbol of leaving torment behind for the young Ilyich.

"I've wanted to steal one of these since I was a kid," he said to Mitia, thrusting the sprayer into his trouser pocket.

Ilyich lay down to sleep with satisfaction that night. He stretched out on a large sofa-bed and turned on the green-shaded table lamp. Silence held sway in the mayor's office. The soft light fell on a pile of papers, a plate with a spoon and the purloined sprayer. He looked at his trophy momentarily and childishly, and, with contented security shining on his face, immediately fell asleep.

Ilyich awoke the following morning in a thoroughly bad mood. Throughout the night he had dreamed that a dentist with vast, bucket-like hands was trying to grab him. He was a small boy again and ran through the city; he hid behind trees and the old five-storey residential blocks. The Godzilla-like dentist stomped its paws along the tarmac, leaving deep footprints. The feeling of security left Ilyich, he felt something clawing at his soul and life seemed tedious and futile again. Angrily, he locked away the sprayer in its box in his desk as Mitia entered the office to tell him that today was an open day when citizens could come to see the commander.

"Oh, yes, I almost forgot. People need our care," chuckled Ilyich, wearing the same smile he had flashed when he cremated the parrot.

Chills ran down Mitia's spine.

At midday they began to receive citizens. A very, very old lady was the first to appear. Mitia struggled to explain to her that the city now had a military commander instead of a mayor.

"What kind of a comedian? Petrosian or who?" the visitor asked.

"Be quick, Granny, do you need something?" Ilyich interrupted.

"I do need, I do need something," the elderly Rovenky inhabitant said, nodding expressively.

She began her tale, which began in 1938. Ilyich, hearing the date, waved his hand to indicate that Mitia should sit because it would be a long story. She continued. When she was little she had loved to go to the small park by her house where there was a pear tree laden with as many fruit as there were stars in the sky; the pears were so sweet, like honey, and the size of fists.

"Grandma, get to the point," the commander grumbled, and wondered whether he should extract his sprayer from the desk to calm his nerves.

"To the point, point, aha, aha," the visitor nodded, wiping her mouth with the edge of her scarf as she continued her story.

The pear was continually sprouting new boughs. Her mother, Avdotia Sviridovna, cursed the child's fascination with the park and compelled her daughter to tear off the boughs. Then…

Ilyich's hand extended towards the box in his desk with the sprayer. After a minute he could not resist, he pulled it out and touched the rubber bulb, smiling brightly. Her narration had become a full blown novella in the interim. Her mother had died, then the war came. The Fritzs came to eat the pears, then the Red Army; then there was the victory. The NKVD came and took away her father who had been a POW. Then industrialisation; a new pear tree grew. She married and then her children went to gather pears. Then they all died except for her. Then another pear tree grew; only to be hewed down by the Cossacks.

He realised, as he jolted back to awareness, that the old woman had come to complain about the damned freaks that had taken away her beloved tree. He had lost the thread of her narrative, having gone into a trance while toying with his dental apparatus. Her talk about the present brought him back to reality. He stood, straightened his jacket and announced solemnly that, "We will put this right."

A decree appeared in the local press later that day:

Neither members of the self-defence units nor Cossacks have the right to simply enter your home and take anything away. If you see that a man is hungry, you may give him a loaf. None of our men, especially those from our high command, will enter gardens, orchards or shops. If you see men dressed in this fashion and acting in this way call us immediately - this is banditry.

Ilyich decided to end his citizens' reception after this decree and find a way to vary his lifestyle.

"Listen Mitia, take me to the mine. I'm interested in having a look," he said to his deputy.

"Of course boss. You find out about life in Donbas from within, we'll organise it," Mitia replied with rapid enthusiasm.

In a couple of hours Ilyich was donning a miner's helmet in the dirty section of the mine's changing room. He was not himself. Naked men wandered around him and the bathing attendants walked nearby without looking at them; used to the sight of many nude miners. In the clean section of the changing room he removed his camouflage fatigues, covered his genitals with his hands and walked down the corridor, with his bare back-side on show, to the dressing room. He donned a boiler suit and received a miner's lamp and breathing apparatus before following Mitia to the pit head. His deputy was now in his native element. The mine, rather than any tedious office business, was his real life. Every other worker they met greeted him. Mitia walked confidently along the corridor and knew every twist and turn so well he could have recognised them if he were blindfolded. He had very often slithered along the corridor blind drunk and almost crawled from the baths into the lamp storage room.

Ilyich stood by the lift bravely and sombrely. Miners can spot from afar anyone who is descending into the pit for the first time. They resemble tourists roaming through a forest. The colliers looked at the commander and hid their smiles. Then everyone entered the lift and the operator gave the signal to descend. Mitia had arranged with the operator to have the lift halt during its descent. The operator lowered it gently and then after a minute braked gently a couple of times. The cage descended for a further minute before the operator slammed on the brakes. The commander went as white as the helmet he was wearing.

A mine lift falls at sixty kilometres an hour, but the narrow shaft and the lift's movement generate air turbulence and create the feeling of flight. Any sudden movement of the lift generates fear in a novice. In addition, the lift, when the brakes are applied, swings upwards and downwards due to inertia. American miners, with their superior facilities, would have enjoyed the Ukrainian mine's fairground attraction effect.

"It's okay," grumbled Ilyich, gripping the handrails with white knuckles. His helmet was skewed to one side. The waistband of his pants had also slipped, and his lips trembled slightly. All his bravado had disappeared in an instant. The lift descended again, but had barely moved before the brakes were applied. Ilyich now realised the true essence of a miner's existence. Standing in the lift on trembling legs, he felt like a tightrope walker on a high wire. It seemed that his life could end abruptly at any moment. He had never felt so defenceless. All his childhood dental reminiscences were nullified before this genuine fear.

He gripped the handrail while Mitia smiled, barely noticeably. The commander was doubled up with discomfort as he walked out of the lift with a drunkard's gait. He entered the pitch darkness as his deputy propped him up. "Let's go Ilyich, I'll show you the coal face."

If Ilyich, who agreed mutely with a nod of his head, knew to what he had consented he would have asked to be shot where he stood. They went to a platform near the electric-powered wagons, took their seats and moved off. The commander grew weaker. A lamp from the aperture of the platform shone after them, the arch of the tunnel glittered, puddles, pipes and miners moved with the motion, like in a metro. The stop came. The commander and his deputy exited the carriage on to a sloped mine working.

Mitia thought of another prank to play on his chief; he led him to the coalface via the longest most arduous path, through a poorly ventilated working. This contained the conveyor belt that carried coal to the surface and it generated coal dust, which hung in the atmosphere. The air was stale, depleted of oxygen and at a high temperature it was sometimes difficult for the miners to catch their breath. They yearned only to sit and breathe, but they had to move.

Ilyich left his jacket fastened even though sweat poured off him like spring rain. Miners never stay buttoned up, they usually leave their jackets unfastened and even work in their underpants occasionally for some salvation from the heat. Ilyich tugged at his breathing apparatus and coughed like an old man; he was drenched like a bath sponge and barely moved. The lift now seemed to be a childish diversion. In this part of the mine the trick was to walk with the barest motion of the legs. When the commander pleaded for some respite from Mitia, the latter shook his head - just hold on a little bit more. It transpired that the 'bit' was a forty-five degree slope and they had to climb up its bumpy, rocky surface. Ilyich underwent a personal Armageddon now. He was on all fours, clinging to odd corners, arched edges, hollows and ledges like a proper mountaineer. They ascended almost one kilometre in this manner. Climbing this kind of working would test even a strong man. The weight that had to be carried and the ascent upwards at such an angle made his legs tremble. His breathing was restricted and his throat spasmed, choking him, but on he went with his load, the lamp, breathing apparatus, and a litre of water.

Barely moving forwards and incessantly straightening his mask, Ilyich wondered how people could toil in such conditions and if it was slave labour. *How could people work thus in the twenty-first century?* The third hour of his time in the pit passed as they laboured upwards. His eyes were popping out of his head with the strain. He fell several times and risked rolling down the slope. He spat, cursed and almost wept. Mitia had already bounded up the slope and laughed while he waited for Ilyich. He watched the light of the commander's lamp approaching from far below. It trembled, lurched from side to side, then ascended again. Half an hour more passed before the white helmet of his boss loomed at Mitia's side.

"AAAAAA OOOOOO, I … you … back home," the commander finally managed to squeeze out the words and spat on the ground. He lay on the floor and occasionally looked down where the working, black as the interior of a gun barrel, fell away below him. It seemed like the darkness of hell swirled down there.

Chapter Ten

According to councillor member, Natalia Maksimets, stray dogs are devouring the corpses of dead Ukrainian soldiers near Luhansk, which the locals have refused to bury. The Luhansk councillor cited the testimony of eyewitnesses, who are residents of Velyka Verhunka. Velyka Verhunka is near to Chervonyi Yar, where the junta tried to break through the LPR lines and lost scores of men. "We bury our own soldiers in gardens because we cannot reach the cemetery due to the shelling by those Ukrainian vipers. No one wants to touch these cursed fascists, so the dogs are tearing them apart." These are the words of a local resident, as quoted by Maksimets.

Report by the Novorossiya Militia, 15.07.2014

Two people moved carefully through the dense undergrowth of the tree plantation. Explosions rumbled in the distance and a machine gun barked in short bursts, akin to a chained dog. The scorched carcass of an armoured vehicle sprawled liked a dragon exhaling fumes. The poplars lining the road vainly tried to shield themselves from the smoke with their leaves. The dark ashes ascended, splintering the rays from an oppressively bright sun, which, now at its zenith, witnessed the battle.

"Dad, what will we do?" the younger soldier, with a St. George's Ribbon fastened to the sleeve of his jacket, asked his companion.

They were both lying in the greenery. The battle was almost over and their unit had fallen into an ambush by the 'Ukies'. Almost all had died and some had fled. The commander had been slain and their armoured vehicles were crippled. The 'Dad', a wiry man with big hands, hugged his AK rifle and tensed in the tangled vegetation. At that moment he wanted to say, *Son, this is the end*, but something bustled behind them. They both jolted and the younger man childishly squeezed the

90

grenade in his hand. A gruff voice said, "Lads, it's me, Anton, call sign, Artist."

After another ten seconds the branches parted and the two militiamen lying in the clearing were joined by a third. Anton's camouflage jacket was scorched in a few places and there was a superficial, ten centimetre gaping wound on his leg; a bullet had grazed his hips. A ragged wound from an explosion bled from his forehead. However, his face, smeared with mud, ash and unknown substances, beamed.

"Well men, you've survived? Don't these fascists aim that well?" Anton asked the question with some delight as he looked at his comrades, who were in fear for their lives.

"So, Artist, you're grinning there, on civvy street you probably just drew naked birds and now you're playing at war," Dad said, looking askance at the newly arrived soldier.

Anton did not reply; he had noticed a human figure through the foliage. Laying a finger on his lips, he pointed towards it. Stooping carefully, he began to weave along a narrow path through the branches of shrubbery. Having advanced ten metres, hidden by the tangled greenery, he saw that the figure was a fighter from a Ukrainian volunteer battalion. He clearly thought that the skirmish was over and none of the foe remained, so had taken a leak. Now he was roaming the plantation without anxiety or, pausing occasionally, just checking out the area. The Ukrainian soldier passed through the bushes where the militiaman sat, and stood with his back to him. Anton took his chance, leaped from the vegetation and smashed his rifle butt into the back of the soldier's head. The soldier fell unconscious, face down in the grass.

Cautiously approaching the enemy, he flipped over the Ukrainian volunteer's body. Nikolai Nikolaev, the man he had saved by beating him off the charged trolley poles in the mine, lay before him. He looked closer, not believing his eyes; yes, it really was his former mining colleague.

They had become friends after the incident. If their shifts coincided they often travelled home together. He had told Nikolai about his pictures and Nikolai had told him about his children and his wonderful wife; they had lived together for fourteen years and if they argued it was only about who loved whom the most. Anton was a little jealous of his colleague. There were a couple of occasions when Nikolai's wife and children came to the bus stop to meet him and the impression he formed was that they were an ideal family. Once Anton had brought Nikolai home and showed him a painting he had made of his friend.

"What? That's me? No one has ever so precisely conveyed my spirit," Nikolai, or Kolia as his friends called him, said enthusiastically.

"You are contemplative, you understand the depths that exist within the superficial smears of personality; the depths from where humanity's essence emerges," Anton had explained.

His former friend was now his enemy. Anton called over the other militiamen and they bound Nikolai and hauled him, like sailors drag a boat overland, to a small, wooden hut. It resembled a suburban dacha in which gardeners store a few tools and was furnished minimally with desks, wardrobes and drawers. They broke down the door and entered. The militiamen hung the volunteer soldier from the roof and sat while they decided what to do with him. It was a long way to their base and what could they use to drag him on was the only question. They did not consider letting him go. The older man said that Nikolai Nikolaev was a volunteer from the Donbas battalion, which had killed many militia and periodically raided their bases and destroyed the equipment of the Russian brigades and the Novorossiya army. The entire battalion consisted of Russian speakers, who were drawn from the local Ukrainian patriots. This disturbed the leadership of the DPR and LPR, who had prophesied that all of Donbas would rise against the junta.

The trio agreed that the younger man and older man would go to seek assistance and transport while Anton would guard the captive. They departed, leaving the former comrades together. Nikolai hung from the ceiling with a gag in his mouth. Anton sat on an old red sofa, the springs of which grumbled irritably. He looked around the room. It contained spades smeared with soil, a hoe, and a green waterproof coat on a nail driven into the wall. A vase with dried meadow flowers stood on a table. This composition evoked a desire to sketch in Anton. He took out his pad and drew the outline around the white spaces with broad strokes before pencilling in the details. "Forsaken life or the withered atoms of the universe," he said as a name for his, as yet, unfinished picture.

In reply, Nikolai groaned through the gag. He saw his old friend spread out on the sofa with his arms resting on his back. He seemed to know who he was looking at and read the desire to draw in his eyes, but it also seemed that this person now sitting in a camouflage uniform with bruises on his face was incomprehensible to him. Life had repainted everything in his personal universe.

"Eee arrr wattttt waannnt," Nikolai murmured.

His foe looked attentively at him, and spent a few seconds checking he was tied securely before he withdrew the gag. The prisoner breathed deeply through his mouth. Anton stepped back a little, demonstratively laying an AK rifle and a large notched knife on the table.

"Why do you need them? Why are you fighting against your own people?" he asked, and sat down on a chair, the white paint of which was flaking. Nikolai raised his eyes and for a moment their gazes met in a silent duel. Two foes, two former comrades; one of whom was indebted to the other for his life, the other finding respite in the man he had saved. Now both were on opposing sides in a war.

"That which they are building now in Russia has no

relationship to the Slavonic world, to the 'Russian Spring', nor to the USSR. They want to implant it in Ukraine too … it's a mixture of orthodoxy and fascism … this is all wrong," Nikolai said.

"All wrong?" screeched Anton. "Do you know that in Lviv the Berkut fighters were made to kneel and then sent to atone by spilling blood in the east. So many of them arriving at the front immediately go over to the side of the militia. Their decision is motivated by this public humiliation. So, what are we talking about. Who is the fascist?"

The captive lowered his eyes. He seemed to be seeking the words and phrases to reach the other man and slip, as quietly as a mouse, through some chink in his closed heart.

"Anton, do you remember how you saved me? Am I your enemy? When we made our way through the workings, when you supported me so I didn't fall, you showed empathy. How could I have changed? The local authorities have supported this. The crime bosses, the 'Regionals', used city mayors and people, shipping them in from all over the province, to create pro-Russian meetings until a chain reaction occurred. This is of course a problem born in the midst of the province itself. And Russia has joined in, dividing the sheep and the rams. Were we enemies? Are we?" the soldier hanging from the ceiling yelled.

Anton listened to his heart, searched for some current of logic, some sense which would allow him to answer this question honestly. Not in reply to Nikolai but for himself. The air tensed as if the destiny of the world was being determined here.

He wanted to say, *Kolia, you are not my enemy. How could you be my enemy if I stood between you and your death?* Whether his salvation of the other man was a deed of little importance was irrelevant, Anton felt some thread connecting him to Nikolai.

"You could change everything. You cannot fight for

fascists. Did our grandfathers fight for them?" Anton asked.

"My grandfathers fought for Ukraine in the soviet army. You say, 'our grandfathers fought'. I'm forming the impression they fought in the ranks of the secret police. Heroic forebears could not have descendants who torture, murder and kidnap," replied Nikolai.

Anton, barely restraining himself and strode around the room, counting his steps like the secondhand of a clock measures time. *Couldn't Nikolai see what was going on? How can I do anything with him? What was to be done?* His heart fluttered from his breast. It seemed that his soul was hanging on the rope with Nikolai. All the weight of the past pulled upon that rope, it trembled and stretched with the tension, then contracted again. Life hung in a fragile balance. Anton suddenly snatched up the knife and raised it to Nikolai's throat. He drew it slowly over the other man's skin so that droplets of blood oozed from tiny lacerations. "One movement separates someone from death. You are brave, for you think you know me. Are you not afraid of death?" He could find no other argument he could use.

The prisoner was terrified now. His whole body tensed and fear swung through his psyche. It would only take one word and nothing would stop the man who was now his foe from taking his life.

"I understand this will sound laughable when said with a knife to my throat, however, that which you do now is a deeply personal choice for me. Perhaps I am a romantic, but I wanted to help my country, so that it becomes closer to the dream that many had on the Maidan," said Nikolai slowly.

Anton was searching for some words, some suggestions, but his comrades burst through the door. They had arrived in an armoured car, ready to transport the prisoner to their base. One of the militiamen severed the ropes from which the prisoner was suspended and the ties binding his feet so he could walk. It was a bright summer's day, the azure porcelain of sky was slashed with attenuated long wisps of cirrus cloud. A bird flashed over the field. It was a flickering point of life that composed its schedule from chance meetings and separations. Then a rumble came, followed by a short burst of fire. An explosion followed and the armoured vehicle burst into flames.

"The Ukies are laying everyone out tak..." the militiaman leading Nikolai managed to cry before collapsing wordlessly.

A sniper was at work. The prisoner darted aside quickly. The Ukrainians had observed the troops who had captured their commander and were ready to devastate everything. Anton, stooping as the bullets whistled overhead, tore after the escaped prisoner. Nikolai hid in the bushes and only a soft rustling gave away his movements. Anton saw his jacket flickering through the greenery. The path meandered through the roadside shrubbery and it seemed the prisoner would soon be out of sight. Nikolai suddenly tripped and rolled into a small ditch. Anton swooped on him as he rose. Both bodies rolled noisily on to the floor. Holding Nikolai's tied hands with one hand, he held the notched knife against his throat. He pressed slightly and droplets of blood covered the glittering blade.

"One move and I'll kill you," Anton warned him. Nikolai froze for a second, but then the footsteps of approaching separatists were heard. This was Nikolai's last chance, a chance like that of a terminally ill patient to be cured. He thrust his whole body towards Anton in an attempt to shrug him off with his legs. His attempt was a single, three-second movement; the sum of the muscles of his back, arms and legs. It should, with mathematical certainty, have produced a result. He had to take the risk now to evade captivity, torture and a shameful protracted death.

The movement did not work out how he had wanted it to. Within the first second of Nikolai's movement Anton had grabbed the prisoner's hands, then he braced his legs to take the blow with the muscles of his back. The third second was the longest.

Anton would later replay the scene in his mind and sometimes that moment returned to him in nightmares. The Ukrainian had almost broken free, twisting like a snake, when a knife had entered his back and its point pierced his breast. At the moment when the skirmish flared, another militiaman saw that the enemy had almost won and immediately stabbed Nikolai, shearing through his torso. Blood sprayed on Anton's face; it was warm, almost like water from a shower. Nikolai's body spasmed once as he died. His former friend, whose life he had saved at the risk of his own life in the mine, someone to whom he had revealed the secrets of the soul and had felt some unfathomable attraction between their spirits, now lay dead. Anton breathed heavily as blood dripped from his face and he felt the curse of his friend's death.

When they returned to the camp that day Anton washed and then washed again to remove the remnants of Nikolai's blood from his face, before reporting the destruction of a dangerous enemy to headquarters. Then he lived a quiet life for a period; the war did not affect him much in the depths of Novorossiya. However, his feat, the capture of a commander they had long hunted for, was noted by the commander of the Army of the South-East and he was awarded the St. George's Ribbon and promoted to company commander.

A few days later, as he passed along the line of troops he commanded, it suddenly occurred to Anton that he could never have imagined himself like this; wearing camouflage fatigues, draped with ammunition belts, fulfilling a role allocated to him by fate. He entered his tent and looked at the picture hanging in its centre. It was his latest work and the one he most valued, an original creation executed in black and white. He wondered when he would have the chance to sit by the canvas again. He only stared at the picture briefly, then remembered what he wanted to do now. He opened his tablet and composed an email:

Sergei, I'm alive. I'm waging war against Ukraine. You may not understand me, but everything has changed for us. This will be a just country.

His hand hung over the 'Enter' key for a few seconds as he thought about whether he should reveal his new life. His family had not known where he was since he had joined up, and for some reason he had a strong sense that he should tell Sergei first. His khaki-clad form hung above the tiny monitor in a comically hesitant pose. He just had to tap the key, but that downward pressure was more than just the application of force. At that moment life was devoid of punctuation, of any personal meaning, or any of his past setbacks; it was a fixed point which would not move or would only shift under the compulsion of other factors. A fluorescent lamp cast its light on Anton's figure, illuminating him against the grey-green backdrop of the tent as his finger pressed the key. A characteristic click and the email hurtled towards its address.

A new person raised his finger from the key; the company commander known as 'Artist'.

Chapter Eleven

In Luhansk, the LPR militants are selling 'expropriated' cars at prices of between UAH 3000-5000. The terrorists have organised a market on Oboronna Street in the centre of the city. They have seized a car showroom and are displaying cars for sale that have been requisitioned from the population. The cars for sale are of European and Chinese manufacture. Some of the machines are without number plates and have been stolen from car showrooms in the city. The militants have now released the owner of the city's Toyota dealership, whom they had previously kidnapped. He had been held for some weeks until he agreed to 'transfer' ownership of the business and its assets to the militants. New, imported cars are being sold for UAH 3000-5000. There are approximately one-hundred vehicles on display at the showroom and its grounds.

An item on the informator.lg.ua site, 06.07.2014

The spacious office, partitioned into a maze of cubicles, was almost empty. The whole room resembled an island. The tops of cabinets, the skeletal cliff faces of monitors and chairs resembled strange, frozen kangaroos. Only one rectangular workplace was dimly lit by a lamp; Sergei was sitting here, he was looking at his monitor and browsing the news.

Once, sitting in a Kyiv café with Yulia Petrenko, whom he had met at a business lunch when he had flown back to Ukraine, they had talked about how the western world provided a comprehensible social structure and a logically organised society. They had debated how to resolve the situation in East Ukraine. Yulia was a shapely, well-toned woman of thirty. Sergei had the impression that her face had been sculpted by angels.

"You must understand," she said, "that the inhabitants of smaller cities and towns in Luhansk province live almost in serfdom. There, a man's worth is judged by how many hours he has worked at the factory or mine. Everything is constructed so that people have no money to travel, indeed, they are not accustomed to travelling and have no need to do so. You broke away, but such successes are rare. Consider where they have the option of going when there is armed conflict on their home territory, and beyond that the threshold of a vast, unknown world."

They went to the riverside area of the Dnipro during the evening. The wind from the river played like a child with Yulia's light-auburn hair. Sergei walked by her side, occasionally looking at her and thinking that he was drawn to her by a feeling he did not recognise. He had lived in Germany for six months and they often corresponded, but rarely met. Now, every time she said something it seemed profound, and a compelling desire to embrace her arose inside him. He wanted to hold her as tightly as he could. This desire had surely arisen out of solitude, although perhaps there was a true woman before him, alongside whom any man would become conscious of himself as a husband and father.

He looked at the cupid's bow of Yulia's lips as her hand straightened her hair. People were sitting on the steps which led down to the water, where a solitary seagull looped and zigzagged. Their conversation entered the vast prairie of the Slavic soul.

"History is much more convenient than the present. You can turn to it at any moment, like turning on a tap, and it's easy to strengthen or weaken the flow," Sergei said.

"Living in the past bores me. Living in 'the country that we have lost', 'the war that we won', 'the grass that was green'. The past continuously sets the agenda in Russia and Ukraine. The struggle for a beautiful past limits any possibility of thinking about the future. Like an argumentative wife or mother who has given her best years to another time, we are incapable of comprehending our present. We don't want to

100

think about what awaits us in the future," she replied.

"There are so many words continuously said about the Banderites. It feels as if Stepan Bandera were still alive," Sergei continued.

"Yes, Ukraine and Russia have very different contemporary histories, but we cannot excuse and close our collective past. We have to calmly acknowledge our history; it will allow us to take a step into the undetermined future, which it is important to meet face on and not with your back turned," Yulia reflected.

At that moment Sergei paused and reflected that Yulia was like a mirror in which he saw his true image. If she were to like him, he knew he must begin to change himself, but in a way that reflected his essence. He halted and gently grazed her cheek with his lips. She smiled and her eyes reflected Sergei's smile.

As he shook his head, he tried to cast the fragments of this memory from his mind. He had long understood that he loved Yulia, but how could he tell her. She lived in Kyiv, worked as a journalist, and had no wish to leave the country; a factor that was a continuous source of arguments and misunderstandings between them.

Sergei's gaze swept over the rigid terrain of the office, with its irregular curves, jagged angles and the desolate rifts of working spaces between desks and chairs. He reflected that he was alone in his life. Someone was always near, he talked with people continuously, but he felt as if he had fallen into emptiness. He had the ties with his family in Rovenky and his connection to Yulia, but these two threads could not completely tie off the wound of his solitude. His monitor flashed suddenly; an email from Anton. Sergei gasped involuntarily after he had read the message, *his brother was alive, but what had he written? What was this just country?* He immediately banged out a reply on the keyboard:

Sergei hit the send button and stared into the monitor, where he saw the horizon of another world.

The following day Artist and his company embarked on a mission to purge the territory to the north of Luhansk, where the 'Kyiv Junta' bases were situated. The APC, smeared with long camouflage stripes and decorated with the symbols of the LPR, St. George's Ribbons and a flag, a couple of tanks and some trucks set off early in the morning. A translucent haze blanketed the line of the forest in the distance. The fabric of the road, pitted with large potholes, gleamed like egg-white in the dawn. The sun had barely risen over the horizon, like an old man pulling on a coat composed of hirsute pale sun-rays. Artist sat on the APC and looked at the faces of his comrades; one was smoking a cigarette and the cloud of smoke trailed the column and dissipated into the acidic atmosphere. His cousin, Yaroslav, a big, burly man, was here. They had met up again after they had both joined the militia army.

"Yarik, how are you, no one's had a go at you?" Artist joked.

Yarik gave a wry grimace in reply, as if he had drunk some harsh-tasting hooch. Life had dragged him by his hair and the scruff of his neck from one lamentable incident to another.

At his first wedding he had become so drunk that he had fallen into the side salad at the reception; his wife drank throughout their marriage and had disappeared one evening. One week later she had turned up and looked unkempt and aged through her short time away; he never knew where she had been.

He was more fortunate with his second wife and they had a child after their first year of marriage. He moved from the auxiliary section of the mine to the tunnelling section; a move workers often make in a Ukrainian mining town. The birth of the child had compelled him to recalculate the budget, wipe away the tears, and seek more money. Poverty was a dragging dull, almost agonising, way of life for many in the provinces. A few thousand hryvnya, an apartment, which was usually rented, and only limited parental help. Like hundreds of people in these areas he had languished in this scenario, sharing a similar fate, as if his life were a duplicate of theirs.

Life in the tunnelling section tempers and cauterises people. These workings are only ventilated by small fans, which stream air along fabric tubes from outside the mine to the tunnel end, however, these fans often draw on air from inside the mine in violation of safety rules. The tubes are often torn and only a small amount of air reaches the coal face, where the temperatures reaches over forty degrees. Yaroslav, like many tunnellers, had often worked while wearing only his underpants, a helmet and a strap with the power pack for his lamp.

He had once been hauling a two-hundred kilogram section of metal guttering to the conveyor. Stopping for a moment he pressed his back against the side of the workings, then he spat and picked up the guttering, hoping to get there faster. He heard a horrible crunching sound as if someone had fallen from a tree. Later he found out he had cracked his vertebrae and torn the muscles in his back. He had pulled with such force that the injuries compelled him to spend one month in hospital. This was heavy, occasionally inhuman slave labour and all for an insignificant two to three thousand hyrvnya each month.

Yarik was still in Rovenky when the front line reached the town. Explosions were heard periodically. Not far from him, a missile fell on a private house and killed four civilians. The local paper printed photographs of parts of the missiles fuselage alongside an old woman wearing a faded dress-apron and with her bare feet in galoshes. As they descended into the pit, the miners always talked about the rumours, tales and news.

"Hear me," said an old tunneller, nicknamed Granddad, as he nudged Yarik. "They say that Kolomoiskyi has located two hundred Grad missiles at the Donbas border. He says it needs cleaning up, fuck this Donetsk lot."

It was like that every day. Human anger, genuine human wrath, accumulated drop by drop, filling the human soul to capacity, and it left no room for another viewpoint or logical argument.

"They have surrounded us and want our surrender?" Yarik screamed at his wife, before joining the militia. "Understand this, I have to go and protect my land; I'm a man with enough in me to tear them apart where they stand."

Yarik later told Artist what he had said to his wife. He refused the pay due to a militiaman. Now they were driving along a rural road, the APC jolted and Yaroslav gripped his right-hand jacket pocket. It held a photograph of his five year old son, who was wearing a spiderman suit, taken one morning during a children's party at the kindergarten.

There was Roma, call sign Skinny, a lazy merrymaker who drank too much and was as lean as a lamp post. He continually scratched his arm where a wound had still not healed. He was unemployed when he joined for the money, an amount of four hundred dollars each month. However, he was now engulfed by an unstoppable desire for vengeance on the Ukrainians.

The militia ran into an ambush again on the day of their expedition.

Artist was sitting on the left hand side of the APC when bullets whistled past him and an explosion boomed. A Ukrainian sniper took out Yarik first. His body rolled, like a heavy, flaccid sack, over the side of the APC. Artist immediately leaped from the APC and that was what saved him. A second later the sniper's next victim was Skinny, who fell like a log on to the asphalt. The APC halted. In front of them, just around a sharp turn, their road was blocked by felled trees. Artist darted towards Yarik. The dark-brown, deep wound left by a bullet to the temple left no possibility of even a glimmer of life. However, his eyes, like the headlights of a car as they are turned off, still gleamed with some living presence; as if pleading for help. They held a frozen image of a boy stretching out his hands towards dark shadowy forms. A second passed and Artist saw only a dead glassiness in his cousin's gaze. A wave of hatred surged within the unseen material of Artist's soul. His world had been flipped upside down. He had known Yarik since he was five years old and now he was gone. Every day the door into the past he had once inhabited was closing by a centimetre at a time. He would have darted towards the reptiles attacking his column, but two tanks in their column beat off the assault.

Artist returned to his tent late in the evening. Two desires battled within him. Part of him wanted to check his inbox, while the other desired only to collapse on to his bed. The desire to read his emails triumphed and he threw himself into his chair while scanning the message from Sergei. A picture emerged before him. Bloodied hands trembling a little, the knife twitching with the tension; drops of blood, like juice oozing from crushed grapes, fell on the earth, lost within the blackness like a tribute, dues, or taxes paid to the treasury of nothingness. Dust to dust. Nikolai's head was laid before him.

Have I killed? Get this, west and east Ukraine have completely different roots. They have different histories and different heroes. They have different conceptions and different ways of thinking. And while there was no issue raised about the differences, there was no conflict. Now someone has played on that division and there are two paths before us - Cutting off our root or dispersing. But this is just one drop in the cauldron that is now seething. I did not go to the west Ukrainians, to their homes, but they have invaded us, so I kill them.

He signed his email 'Artist' and unhesitatingly pressed the 'Enter' key before falling asleep.

The correspondence continued in this way for over a month. Every time Sergei appealed to Anton's intellect, his younger brother replied that it was a war for the future. They could not live as they had done in the mines and be old at fifty. Where could he find meaning in such a life if it had none, so he needed to take charge and build his own future. Sergei replied from Munich, using strange verbal metaphors in an attempt to reach his brother:

In the formation of your existence now, everything is concentrated on the point of 'here and now'. So your life flows along, balanced on the sharp end of a knife point. The individual only sees and hears really within a brief moment of the million-faceted totality of time. This property is static. This way of being is therefore going nowhere and unbeing approaches it down the incline of life's events. We do not essentially approach death, but death approaches us. The individual stands like a pillar in a field towards which the truck of unbeing hurtles at great speed to crush and unify them with nothingness. You have stepped forward to meet that truck. It will crush you and that will be all. And you have children.

He regarded it as important to understand life's rules. Anyone embarking on the ruination of life will receive the far greater ruination of their own existence in response.

We have another country, people have changed hugely; the war and the racket of explosions have done their work. Now they no longer want to live in Ukraine. Have you become so remote in Munich? Don't you understand the current state and conflicts. Some people think that West Ukraine wages war with terrorists and the east of the country wages war with the fascists in power. Perhaps this is a contrived scenario, or perhaps a concurrence of circumstances and an apt reaction to them. I don't know. We only know what they permit us to know. I expect that, not wishing this myself, I can somehow help you understand and to understand me; I want to understand you, why you are so ardently a devotee and fighter for the national cure? It would be better to meet face to face if God gives us a time and a place for a meeting.

Artist replied and switched off the computer.

Chapter Twelve

The beautiful elegant churches, the houses, the well-tended land, the peaceful region - Today all this is in the past, but it will be restored and revived from the ruins and ashes. The Ukrainian army fired shells and mortars into the Diocese of Rovenky today.

Archpriest Aleksandr Avdiugin, ZhZh, 26.08.2014

A bulb blinked nervously in the chandelier in Ilyich's office. The commander was writing something on A4 paper. He slowly scrawled the symbols and signs with the handwriting of a first grader. Ilyich stuck out his tongue as he concentrated, like he used to do in school. Ilyich, or to give him his correct name, Pavel Reznikov, had done much that should and should not have been done at school, but mostly the latter. While in fourth grade, during an argument, he had driven a ten centimetre nail into a board and spat on its head; after that he became known as Gvozd, meaning nail.

In the sixth grade, in an attempt to avoid a maths lesson, he stole a bucket of slops from the canteen and tipped it down the stairwell and over his teacher's head. He darted to his classroom even as the fetid mess was swirling through the air to make sure he had an alibi. He would be a legend in his own lunchtime. Alas, the purple borshch-tinged liquid missed its target and doused the headmistress.

"Oh, I really caught it then. I had to kneel in front of the whole school who were lined up to watch. Then my dad gave me a thrashing back at home. I've still got the scars on my arse," Ilyich said aloud as he smiled at this recollection.

The commander's thoughts were interrupted by a knock on the door. Mitia entered, holding a few sheets of printed paper. "I've done as you asked and got on to the guys ... they've written about the situation in the town," his deputy said,

108

flopping into a bright red armchair.

The mayor's representatives usually sat in this chair and there was Mitia throwing his legs, one over the other, like a real cowboy. His satisfied face broke into a smile, as if he had won the jackpot. However, Mitia had obtained something greater in reality. A revolutionary wave had borne him out of a social quagmire; and self-importance was worth far more than money to a man who has been humiliated and oppressed all his life.

"Let's see, let's see," said Ilyich, putting on his spectacles. He hid these glasses from his Cossack brothers, who said that they contained some secret. Whenever they brought him a piece of paper he put them on and studied it as intently as if it were a travel pass.

"Maybe there is a camera in there which relays everything to the Kremlin," an old Cossack, with a memorably proud moustache, had once said to Mitia. Mitia had laughed in reply, twisting his finger by his temple.

Now the usual scene was playing out in the mayor's office. Ilyich - Paper - Spectacles. Mitia looked intensely at the commander, recollecting the moustachioed Cossack. He moved half a metre away from the visual field of the glasses, very carefully. If the Kremlin professionals suspected anything, it would all be over. A knife across his throat and his corpse thrown down a well like in that film.

The secret of Ilyich's spectacles was very simple. They contained plain glass rather than lenses. He wore them to look respectable. He hid them so no one would know of his Batia's wish to look more intelligent.

"Onalytical note," he read aloud, while looking expressively at Mitia from behind his spectacles. Although Gvozd performed poorly at school he knew that 'analytical' like 'annals' is written with an 'a'. Yes, 'annals', he recollected.

The terrified Mitia thought that the KGB were scanning him and flipped up his collar as if chilled. This unexpected movement baffled the commander because it was so airless in the office. Ilyich straightened his glasses, put on a sombre expression and drew his brows into a frown. It was unclear how long these two would have contended over who wore the most serious facial expression, but Mitia was the first to crack. He yelled, indeed almost squeaked, "Keep reading it."

"I'm reading it, don't fuss, you're shrivelling up like my balls on a winter evening," the commander swiftly replied with a smile.

During the fighting in Luhansk, a pumping station was blown up in the vicinity of Molodohvardiysk. As a result there is no tap water in Rovenky. Over two months have passed since the city closed all the Ukrainian bank branches situated there. No ATMs are working and in order to withdraw money people have to travel to Kharkiv, which is three hundred kilometres away. Or to the city of Gukovo, which is nearer and in Russia's Rostov province. The deficit of produce has resulted in a doubling of prices on the local market. All major businessmen have fled the city and most small enterprises are not operating. The mines are beginning to compel miners to take unpaid leave. There is an alarming shortage of bread. Citizens are queueing for bread between four and six o'clock in the morning, but each person is sold no more than two loaves. Those mobile networks that are operating are only doing so poorly; MTS periodically falters and you can only make calls on Kyivstar at night.

"A bad business," Ilyich muttered finally, pulling the glasses from his nose and stuffing them in his pocket. Mitia slumped on his chair like a threadbare teddy bear.

"And, eh, Batia, Russia will help maybe?" he addressed his boss weakly.

Batia groaned. He would have liked to say yes, of course, but there was little news from the handlers in Rostov. They just kept repeating the same thing: "Hold the city, maintain order and, above all, do not let in the National Guard." *What guard? Those who shoot around here are just our mob of marauders.* He had been involved in quite a tussle with Aleksey Mozgovoy, the Commander of the South-East Army, recently. And for what? Our Cossacks had looted a distillery in Krasnyi Luch. Three of them had enter fully armed and told the owner to get them two litre bottles. He told them where to get off. The Cossacks blew their tops, tied the owner to a chair and took as much vodka as they could. Then, already plastered, they went back to Rovenky. Mozgovoy's men stopped them at the checkpoint to find out why they were in such a state. His Cossacks had told them to sod off and had torn past the checkpoint with the guards pursuing them.

The militias around Rovenky were already shooting at each other, firing a couple of rounds from this or that side. The locals heard the AKs popping and thought that Right Sector were attacking. *Let them think that, so they are afraid,* thought Ilyich. *It was too quiet in the town so a curfew is required. Then they could break it on purpose a couple of times.* Recently, the men had set up a mortar near mine number seventy-one and fired it into the field. It was all quiet after eight o'clock, few people went out on to the street, and the shells had boomed so loudly in the field that half the town had heard them.

The lamp winked nervously while the sombre Ilyich remained sitting in the mayor's office. Mitia wagged a foot nervously. Two flies circled the air incessantly, weaving around each other and flying apart in all directions, as if dancing a passionate insect tango.

"I've decided. Let's announce a gathering of the city tomorrow, we will raise their fighting spirit," said Ilyich. He swatted a fly that had settled on the table as his deputy stood. Ilyich, as smug as he was in his schooldays, flicked the fly at Mitia.

The next day the square before the city hall throbbed

with a boiler brought in to warm the crowd during the first cold days of winter. A few hundred people had gathered. A motley crowd as the proudly moustachioed Cossack would have said, but no one asked him and he never spoke without the need. That is how he had been taught to carry himself in a Russian area not far from here. The Rovenky citizens chattered as if they were at a party in a kindergarten.

"The Americans are to blame, they've incited this war and their henchmen in Kyiv have sold out for dollars, the Ukrainian economy is eaten up with debt," an old woman said briskly to her neighbour, while putting on her headscarf.

"Aha, we are holding out. Moscow wasn't built in a day. The main thing is we'll live without oligarchs and fascists. Russia will soon start giving us money in roubles. So what, the main thing is we'll survive. We'll have gas while Kyiv freezes," a skinny, short-haired woman chimed in.

The crowd chatted, but all were waiting for the entrance of their hero, the commander. Rain fell, saturating them from a grey sky that was perforated as if by gunfire. The weather was appalling, but the crowd did not disperse because the people of Donbas had long been bereft of a communal ideal. There was no unifying concept that would have glued society together. No one said, *Let's build a nation state wherein we will be Ukrainians. Or let us become a beacon within the Eurasian world, a beacon of spirituality within 'the Russian World'.*

None of these ideas took root within the Donbas area, there was no soil they could have been sown in; neither did a national liberation nor religious movement because there were too many nationalities. They had driven Russians, Ukrainians, Tatars and Armenians to Donbas after paroling them straight from the penitentiary from 1950 onwards. Old timers remember that out of a ten-man working unit, eight would have been former prisoners. The mining master, their immediate boss, was too scared to say a word out of place to them.

A soviet experiment was conducted in the area during the post war years - ethnic amalgamation. With the exception of a couple of songs about miners, there was no deep, unique culture in Donbas. No system of signs and symbols that would have distinguished the inhabitants of this mining area from the rest of the inhabitants. They, these people, the working class, step monotonously and directly towards the factory or mine. Even teachers kept their origins concealed if they ventured beyond Donbas. De-personalised people lived in de-personalised cities. The soviet powers demanded a typical approach with especial severity in architecture and street names, and the same principles applied to everything. If you were to visit any small town in Luhansk province, you would find no interesting old buildings. This faceless society had been transplanted from the Soviet Union into Ukraine; as if someone had 'copied and pasted' it. They controlled the people and always painted an image of some enemy for them.

So, in 2004, miners were listed and dispatched to meet in Kyiv in support of presidential candidate, Viktor Yanukovych. People were given leaflets with an image of Ukraine divided into 'normal' and 'fascist' areas. This collective social mood was occasionally brought to the boil like a kettle on a hob. It was not surprising then that some of the people of Donbas wanted first and foremost to be separated from Kyiv. They felt an acute need to imbue their collective ego with meaning. Then the idea of a just society, without fascists or oligarchs, emerged. No one was concerned by the fact this idea was ferried from Kremlin offices in a folder, having been developed by Russia analysts. No one worried about that, on the contrary, many residents were again ready to suffer and sacrifice part of their comfort and even to suffer torment. In this they differed from Crimea where life was buzzing under sails swelled by the wind, until it was occupied and the ship was borne by the waves to a half-empty peninsula. Donbas wanted to live beneath the banner of that faith its people had acquired in recent months. They were inclined to become martyrs to that new faith. At the extreme, there were many who were ready to freeze, starve, and sit without water or communication. These inhabitants of Donbas sacrificed themselves to the new world, like Abraham had sacrificed his son, Isaac. However, they hoped that when the knife was poised in the air over their throat, the Kremlin God would act and save the Donbas people.

The inhabitants of Rovenky, who were at the meeting, buzzed with chatter. In some places scuffles almost broke out. Those who dared came to the front of the crowd and yelled something or other into its midst.

Ilyich emerged from the city hall with the stateliness of the cruise ship Aurora leaving its dock; Mitia trotted alongside him. The angry buzzing of the crowd did not abate and seemed set to last for eternity. The commander withdrew his pistol from his pocket slowly, as if it were a sandwich, then he released the safety catch languorously and fired into the air. The crowd was instantly silenced. Ilyich looked around, as if searching for the foe in the masses before him, but there were no foes in their midst. The crowd sensed inwardly that the commander really was as hard as nails. Everyone knew it was better not to anger him, but then an old woman in a headscarf could not stop herself.

"Son, there's been no pension for three months, we're living on flour, only cooking pancakes, when will there be any money?" she blurted, almost pleadingly.

The commander did not move an inch. "Everything will be great, there will be pensions, not yet but later … possibly," he said haltingly.

So, he dished out promises in every direction, while the weary crowd fell silent, ready to believe anything, until he had pledged everything possible. Then he wanted to announce 'to the citizens of a free city' new measures to restore order. He had heard the phrase in a film, but could not remember which.

"Citizens of a free, really free city," he said, reinforcing the metaphor, more to assure himself than anyone else, "the sale of alcohol in the city is restricted to the period between nine hundred and twenty-one hundred hours. If this measure is infringed, punitive measures will be applied under the martial law in force. Our units, without spoiling the relaxed ambience, will enter premises and ensure that the measure is being maintained in restaurants, cafes and bars. If we see a young person drinking beer near a kiosk, we will apply punitive measures under martial law."

The men gawped in dismay, while the old women almost applauded, and the teenagers were plunged into depression. *A revolution is a revolution and what use does it have for alcohol?* However, the provocative Ilyich did not stop the runaway train of revolutionary measures there. He spoke at great length about how he had received a telegram from the Kremlin. All pensioners were summoned to register at the mayor's office and would receive one thousand hryvnya. "Soon citiz…" but then he remembered that what he was about to say required a change of tone. "Soon comrades, the Russian banks will come here and the ATMs will work; soon, literally, we will be revived. You have my word of honour."

Ilyich removed his tatty, greasy cap and crossed himself thrice. Mitia, imitating his boss, crossed himself twice. The old woman, who believed in his charisma, crossed herself once, but slowly and admiringly. When the crowd dispersed, Ilyich roamed around the square for a long time. He kicked up the autumnal leaves gathered there and remembered his teenage years.

A fortnight later, the commander and his deputy were thrown unceremoniously into a basement. Someone in the crowd, probably a devotee of alcohol, had written a slanderous epistle to the Cossack Ataman in Rostov-on-Don. They alleged that the commander was collecting tributes of five thousand hryvnya at a time from businesses and was going to run off with the money. The local men had not liked his new prohibition law. "How can you have a good life and stay sober?" they had asked in bewilderment.

The Ataman had immediately dispatched a telegram to the Kremlin when he received the slanderous missive. They replied with orders to arrest Ilyich and sent a new commander with such a promising name that no one could believe it. Anyone from Rovenky could soon say the new military head's name with pomp and ceremony, Armen Mkrtechevich Mkrtchian. He was a strict man and swiftly incarcerated the previous leadership in revolutionary fashion. There was no need for him to mollycoddle them.

The men muttered among themselves, "Mkrtchian has locked our Ilyich and Mitia in a cell in the basement."

In truth they did not clarify whether Mkrtchian was a name, nickname or a title. It was all the same. The ex-commander sat in a cell with autumn's darkness and cold surging through the wire mesh of his window. Mitia had a drink straight after they had thrown him down into the basement. He had always managed to find alcohol every day; a talent enjoyed by professional alcoholics. Ilyich approached the window occasionally, donned his spectacles with the plain glass and moved his lips. No one knew what he said. Only the occasional passers-by who ran past the basement said that they heard some muffled voice talking endlessly about reviving the town.

Chapter Thirteen

Reports have emerged on the internet of the plans by members of the DPR and LPR to issue their own currency. "Separatists in Donbas have displayed samples of their own money, which they are preparing to issue as soon as is practicable. The currency has acquired the name 'Chervonets' and is required to be interchangeable with Russian RUB and Ukrainian UAH. However, the old UAH currency must be compulsorily surrendered," according to the announcement of the leaders of so called 'Novorossiya', the report states.

From an item on the Glavnoe site, 20.09.2014

It was early morning and a light, perforated mist, resembling a torn serviette, swirled over the camp of the militants. The whole establishment had the air of a table that had not been cleared. Strewn timber resembled scraps of bread, and bulging wooden huts were like uneaten salad. A chimney pipe from the largest tent exhaled smoke.

Artist loved the morning when nature had a particular lethargy. Dew, cold with the autumn, clung in droplets to the grass stalks and fallen leaves. He saw the slow rhythm of life, as if nature were now set to a slower pace. Every movement seemed fettered with the remnants of sleep. He loved roaming the world at the time when most people still dozed. A few troops wandered around the site and a mangy, stray dog hung around the food tent.

Yesterday, Artist had volunteered to join the assault on Donetsk airport; the 'Ukropi', as they now called the foe, were ensconced there. The Ukrainian troops believed that the airport was the most important strategic base for attacking Donetsk. The fiercest fighting was now taking place there. The airport had been besieged without success for six months by the Russian hybrid army. The Ukrainian parachutists and volunteer units fought fearlessly against the local 'militia', the Russian army and GRU special forces. They had become known as the Cyborgs. The battalion commander had laughed as he explained the situation at the site to Artist.

"The storming of Donetsk Airport is smoothly entering the next phase; the purging of the area from the too arrogant, too stubborn Ukropi soldiers. There are still some underground utility areas where the wildest specimens from the population of blue and yellow nazis will hide for a couple of days ... and then ... Debaltsevo ... this is the most significant transportation node. After the capture of Debaltsevo, the Ukropi military began to pullback. The Ukrainian troops are becoming embroiled in another 'kettle'," said the battalion commander as he adjusted the furry Cossack cap he wore.

The Donetsk trip seemed like a piece of cake to Artist. There had not been a large-scale skirmish locally for a protracted period. The opposing sides were just strengthening their positions and regrouping their forces. So, as he roamed the half-empty camp, looking at the early morning confusion and the seemingly calm soldiers, he thought about going to shoot the Ukropi. He still felt the fatigue of summer's eternal heat, midges and mosquitoes. The long awaited chill of September had now started to engulf everyone, every tent and every object. Artist shivered momentarily; it was time to gather his things and set off.

Three days later he was in the vicinity of Donetsk. The approaches to the airport rumbled with shelling and shots sounded at the rate of one a minute. There was a one-storey building with shattered windows and a fallen tree to the left. A man in camouflage fatigues was prone before three steps to the entrance; it seemed as if he had lain down to bask in the warmth of the sun and felt the breath of life waft over him; his left arm stretched upwards, as if he wanted to lay it under his head as a pillow. His right lay on his stomach. Only one tiny detail negated this idyllic picture: there was a clear, bloodied bullet hole in the centre of his forehead. A sniper had taken him out. The one-day old corpse was now prone on the asphalt in front of the building, with a partially smoked cigarette dangling from his lips. Artist stared at the frozen facial mask of the dead man. Perhaps he had been wanting to get married or, conversely, get divorced when he had been shot. Thoughts flew through his own mind, circling like flies around the axis of his desires. *What did he want?*

"Artist, get down, get down, motherfucker," a young militiaman yelled; there was fear in his eyes. A couple of gunshots sounded in the distance. Artist shook his head, as if to dispel his obsessive reflections. The militiamen ran between buildings, vehicles, the runway, some containers and some fuel tanks parked in their bays. A corpse came into view and they slowed just for a moment. They needed to hurry though before the shooting intensified. Two of them stooped and ran towards one of the larger hangars where the militia were located.

Artist had been assigned to the command of the notorious Motorola, the commander of the anti-tank special forces unit, Spartak. He was famed for his videos of the combat in Sloviansk. In civilian life Motorola had been a car thief from Rostov-on-Don, called Arseny Pavlov. He had served as a marine prior to that and fought on two occasions in Chechnya. He explained his arrival in Ukraine simply: "I got on a train and came. I didn't get what was happening. There are Russians here, so I came. As soon as the Molotov cocktails were thrown at the police on Maidan I understood. This is a war. After the nazis said that they would kill ten Russians for one of their own, I saw no sense in waiting until the threat was realised." He repeated these words quite often.

Motorola was a hero to many of the militia and had received a medal 'For Military Valour - Novorossiya'. The internet went viral over a photograph of his wedding to a long-legged girl who towered over him. However, he had a first wife in Russia whom he had not divorced. Myths and rumours swirled around him. They said that he had once, single-handedly, blown up two Ukrainian tanks. This was the source of his popularity. His face always adorned the social network groups linked to Novorossiya.

As soon as he met him, Artist was impressed by the legendary commander. Motorola was dishing out orders, coordinating intelligence and dispatching his soldiers to fight. Artist saw how the militiamen obeyed him and seemed ready to die for him.

"Tomorrow we will drive out this Ukropi filth and strew the runway with their bodies, like they did with our soldiers. We don't forget and we don't forgive," he screamed into a videocamera before the battle.

The Ukrainian military had strengthened their positions in the old and new terminals. The walls of the old terminal were strong and its roof was calculated to withstand heavy loads. Even mortar shells could not pierce it. However, another storm was planned for the following day and everything might change.

It was evening when Artist arrived at the militia's base at the airport. The troops had kindled a fire in the hangar and a few of them were sitting by the flames; three went out to gather intelligence and five guarded the perimeter. Artist spotted another commander, the Georgian Hiwi, in discussion with Motorola, a small distance from the fire. The cold penetrated the hangar through the damaged door and drifted around every soldier gently, like a wild animal touching its cold paws to their backs and their legs. Artist moved closer to the flames. There were many strangers around who, judging by their accents, were Russians. There were also Abkhasians and a couple of Chechens, but the larger part were local people. The war had helped them find a higher position than they had previously enjoyed. A seventeen-year old soldier was cleaning his AK rifle as he sat; his face was adult and simultaneously childish. They called him Toddler in the division. *What had he seen, what vivid memories did he have of life, apart from the last few months of combat? He had certainly not studied at college and it was unlikely he had a long-term girlfriend. What would his life be after the war?*

A forbidding forty-year old man sat nearby, call sign Chervonets, who looked at the tongues of fire which seemed to be mocking people. It gave warmth but would not let anyone draw close and know its essence. Perhaps Chervonets was counting off, day by day, his past life, like rosary beads: the wedding where his young, curly hair, as buoyant as a wind-bellied sail, moved on his head, or in the army, surrounded by other soldiers, standing in an APC with a backdrop of sand dunes and twisted trees, or going to the factory and stopping near the entrance, looking back gloomily and waiting for someone. People often measure out their past like images in a cinema, in frames, fragments and episodes, as if trying to find a meaning in a picture mazed with cracks, coated in dust and moth-eaten by time.

"Why so gloomy, Artist?" Motorola asked, suddenly patting him on the back.

"Oh I'm just thinking a little about life," Artist replied.

"And what's life? She's like a girl, push her and she'll give way," the commander said, laughing into his red beard.

"Well, sometimes yes, sometimes no. If we admit that life is emptiness then it only appears that she can give us something," Artist replied.

"Like an echo, you've exaggerated things." Motorola paused for a few seconds and then continued, "I'll say one thing to you. Every time I do wet work on these reptiles, I understand that I do not live in vain. If it wasn't for the war what would I do - wash cars? Well, no, I have cleaved open so many Ukropi skulls that I don't count them now. So what? Do they have more brains? Fuck no. We are all the same, them and us. But the difference is I spill their blood and they don't shed mine. I live a man's life. You see it's stupid to decide whether to live or not. This is where the real thrill is."

The other men sat quietly by the fire. It was obvious they were used to the speeches of their commander.

"And what about an ideal? About Novorossiya?" asked Artist.

"Does an ideal hamper you? I am not troubled by one, leave it be." Motorola grinned and threw a piece of wood into the fire, which responded with a glittering wave and sparks as fine as sea spray.

"Don't we want to build another country purer and more just than this one?" Artist persisted.

"We want, we want," said the commander, still smiling. "What justice are you looking for? It is in force now, don't you understand. In our fists. He who is smarter, he who is stronger. Not some fairy tale of the human value or human rights. Look how Putin has been; he bows the whole world to his will. He has seized Crimea and sent the military into Donbas. And what? What about fucking democracy? The right of the strong; that's the idea of Novorossiya."

Artist was dumbfounded and looked a little stunned at Motorola and then at the fire. He saw the world as a building with an idealised structure. It had a well-tended entranceway, neatly painted benches and flowers in the garden. The corners of the building were precise, like the truth of geometry or the truth of perfected human action. If you worked well then the building would glitter with purity. Now it seemed it was possible to burst into an apartment and evict its residents. It was okay when he was fighting the Ukropi, but the war was clearly coming to an end. "The war is coming to an end," he said, repeating his thoughts aloud.

The commander looked at him, his beard glowing yet redder in the glittering firelight. He held a shell fragment, which had become carbonised, in his hands. He resembled a weird steam engine stoker as he threw timber into the flames, smiled or poked the fire.

"No, bro, the war won't end. Never. Even when the explosions cease it will rage here from time to time," Motorola said, tapping his forehead. Then he was silent for a few seconds and continued. "I live with a cow. Do you see her being milked now? Do you think she would have given me any before? No bloody way. You make your own fate whatever you desire. If you want to be a man, grab life by the balls and hold on till you're stuffed with cash."

Motorola would have concluded his life lesson to Artist but Chervonets butted in, slapped his knee and said, "The war will be everywhere, Kyiv, western Ukraine, Europe. I will fight my way to the Pentagon and look through its smashed windows at American corpses."

They fell silent as the night hung leadenly over them. The fire blinked like a gold tooth in the dark mouth of the vast hangar. People flitted like shadows across another fire lit elsewhere in the vast structure. When they stepped back from its flames, as it flared, the red nooses of flame cooled somehow and were as stale as the air over a day-old corpse.

Chapter Fourteen

Doctors at the dermatological/venereal disease clinic in Luhansk, who are working without lighting and salaries, have received canned meat. Employees at the city's STI clinic were obliged to write a statement 'of their own free will' and transfer to the protectorate of the Ministry of Health of the LPR. From 1 September, the medical facility operates under the 'jurisdiction of the republic'. This information was provided by a reliable source. These converts have already received a salary for September. This consisted of canned meat from Yoshkar-Ola, some unlabelled tins of fish, and 50 grammes of tea. "The head doctor dished out these allocations by hand," said the source.

From an item on the informator.lg.ua site, 16.10.2014

The border guard at Boryspil stared at Sergei Nedelkov. He looked him over thoroughly with an air of incredulity and raised his eyes to Sergei's face, as if seeking confirmation of his fears. Finding nothing untoward, he stamped the passport abruptly with a loud thud.

Sergei emerged from the glass façade of the terminal and headed to the nearest taxi. One minute later the Kyiv air thrust through the open window of the car, like a wild beast ruffling the driver's shaggy head. It flowed over the driver's seat and became tame as it gently licked Sergei's face.

He had not visited his homeland for three years and had almost forgotten the morning freshness of Boryspil forest, which filled his lungs and delighted his spirit with its coolness. His feelings were now twofold; the air felt tender on his skin but pierced his chest. War was raging in East Ukraine and he had watched reports from the front every day on the German news. His heart sank at them and was immersed in a pain whose nature, ultimately, he could not explain. He sat in an apartment with a view of a quiet German street through the windows and, seemingly, had no cause to be alarmed. The emails from his brother disturbed him of course, but he had no wish to rush to Donbas and persuade his relatives to change their minds.

That pain did not subside, but flared up in accord with the news from his homeland. That feeling, which had appeared at the beginning of the Maidan, strengthened as he saw the footage of ruined villages and towns in the Donbas area. Sergei tried to fight this oppressive emotion; he watched the news less and went walking through a Munich ablaze with summer. Once he was walking on the pavement and he saw a couple of Russian tourists in front of him. He recognised them, not by their clothes but by their personal appearance. This had nothing to do with their attractiveness or otherwise. What gave them away, like a mask painted with strokes understood in advance, was the oppressive tone. It seemed as if their faces were covered with a dark veil compelling certain behaviours and emotions; the challenging behaviour, loud conversations, sullenness, and sometimes the hatred.

Sergei walked behind them, a man and a woman who were well dressed, middle aged and clearly on an above-average income. The man held the woman's hand while she talked incessantly. She was outraged by the morals of the Germans and referred to the second world war for some reason. Then they saw the cover of *Der Spiegel* on a news-stand, with the headline *Stop Putin Now*. The couple froze and then began talking loudly. "The bitches can't relax about us," said the woman, tapping her companion with her finger.

"Just because Russia has risen from its knees," he said, standing up straight and pausing before saying in a louder than usual voice ,"there are fascists all around, here and in Kyiv."

His eyes met those of Sergei. They stared at each other for ten seconds before the tourist gave Sergei a look of disgust, pulled his wife's hand and walked away. Sergei was startled and did not move. His heart was a pounding motor that seemed about to stall. He suddenly understood his anxiety was due to the collision of two worlds. It seemed like something had caused a fissure within him; into it rolled his carefree life, German tranquillity and calm, measured days. At the other side of that fissure lay his country, torn apart by war, its devastated cities and thousands of victims. He could not conceive of what lay between these extremes or what filled the abyss between them; infinite nothing.

As he looked after the departing Russians he realised that the war was just a reflection of the inner world of these people. *They were transfixed in a time at some point in the late soviet period.* He wondered why this had occurred. *How could intellectuals, who were trained to think critically, suddenly lose all connection with reality? What was propaganda? It was the substitution of words for reality. Words which did not present the real state of things but utterly deformed them. Then the language became like a fog around the individual and it became hard for them to distinguish between falsehood and truth. This mutation of the language had begun in the nineteen twenties. All the words which created illusions, such as as 'Excesses' and 'Enemies of the People' etc. People became accustomed to words without possessing the meaning which they should possess.* Sergei now understood that these origins had led to modern propaganda being so easily accepted via these monstrous permutations in the Russian language.

Every day he remained in Germany added to his compelling feeling of guilt, until ultimately he could not resist the pull of his homeland. Now his car raced along the smooth Boryspil highway and he occasionally glimpsed advertising billboards. He checked into a hotel in central Kyiv and then walked to the Khreshchatyk and looked at the photographs of the Euromaidan protest displayed on the city's central square, Maidan Nezalezhnosti. He walked around the area for a while before he noticed a slim girl in a tight blue dress standing by one of the photograph stands. She stood and stared thoughtfully, not at a particular photograph but at something deep inside it.

"It's as if you want to help them ward off the flames," said Sergei, nodding towards an image of the protestors before a wall of fire.

The girl turned, hesitated momentarily and smiled easily, making it clear they were now acquainted. Her name was Alyna Miahkova; she had a pretty face, full lips and when she smiled her eyes became two dark, glittering almonds. When she laughed she seemed like another person, simple and open. They went to Shevchenko Park in the evening. He told her about his brother and glanced stealthily at how she flinched with each frightening word. It transpired that she was also an artist in the expressionist manner, who mingled feelings within depths of colour.

"Art is the breeze of emotion, even if sometimes it freezes like emotions. Occasionally it seems that the image has always lived outside the author and not within them; that it has dwelt somewhere external, fluttering in the air. The artist only takes and seizes the picture and materialises it," Alyna said seriously as she looked at him.

When she saw how Sergei reflected on her words she smiled and her eyes turned into curved slivers of almond and shone.

He returned to his hotel room later in the evening with a sense of fatality and sat in the armchair while looking at the rectangular window strewn with the lights of the nocturnal city. He was surrounded by the meagre furnishings of the hotel: a bed, a chair, a table. He looked at the glimmering lights as if he wanted to see some order in their chaos, to see that which had never failed. Sergei looked at the city, as if trying to dissolve the darkness with his gaze as his eyes always chanced on the outlines of buildings and residential blocks; their half tones rupturing the gloom, like the pictures painted by his brother. He was unable to sleep for a long time, as he thought about Anton.

Sergei darted out of bed the next morning. He had an appointment to see Yulia Petrenko at ten o'clock and they had not met for many months. He checked for a reply every time he emailed her, but on many occasions she did not respond. Yulia awakened mixed feelings in him. He knew their relationship was very unstable and had realised, only a few months after they had met, that she was married. This revelation occurred by chance when he stumbled across a picture of her with another man on the internet. He had checked the man's profile and saw that Yulia was his wife. That evening he wrote her an angry message criticising her for two timing him. He said his heart was now broken because he really loved her. He received a reply consisting of only three characters: an ellipsis.

He wrote her messages brimming with his feelings more than once. She always seemed to take the role of escaping him, and he the role of the pursuer. She had compelled him to be completely open, but had always maintained a distance, which caused him pain.

He often wrote to her: *Who am I to you? Tell me who I am to you?* In reply he only ever received the short phrase: *A man dear to me.*

He was tormented daily and often talked to her on *Skype*, when their conversations were warm and tender. She was interested in how he lived and his professional success. She entered his life deeply and then disappeared.

"It's not that my husband, Kolia, doesn't love me, but we live in different worlds. I'm in the kitchen corresponding with and chatting to many men on the internet. I have a lot of fans and a dozen or so lovers. Kolia doesn't know for sure, but he can guess all this," she said.

Her world, broken and convoluted, was not acceptable

to her husband. He always condescended to her, not knowing what was in her soul. He was afraid of her internal pain because he could not deal with it. They both lived cocooned in their separate lives. She in the kitchen with her devotees; he in the living room with the television.

"What's more, Kolia's infertile and can't have children. I'd have left him, probably," she said during a video call to Sergei.

Hope blazed in his eyes. Sergei had realised he was in love with her simply enough. A month after they had met he tried to stop seeing her. He wrote her a letter saying they needed to separate because she was married. He tried to tear his compulsion for her from his heart. He had tossed and turned like a wounded animal in his bed throughout the night. He roared like an injured creature and punched his pillow; he could not help himself. He longed to write a conciliatory message because he felt the pain of their separation physically. After a few hours he composed a message and selected her name, with cinematic slowness, in his email address book.

He had separated with her many times after that episode, but the result was the same every time, he always returned to Yulia. On each occasion he had written her a vast epistle in which he had sketched their relationship. She replied in her customary short phrases. She wrote to him about her internal pain that was concealed from everyone and how Kolia was afraid of uncovering that pain; afraid that he would not be able to help her. So he chose to live in a world that was comfortable and comprehensible for himself.

Sergei had once proposed marriage to Yulia. He wrote that he could release her from the cell in which she had locked herself. A refusal followed; then a second; then a third. After six months they had almost ceased communicating, but occasionally he sent her his long, long emails:

All drama is a wound and creativity symbolises the pain of separation between your own ego and the object of your unattainable desire. Perhaps this is how it should be. When experiencing suffering, the individual reflects on the life which exists within that separation. Or perhaps it is not so: life is that which is concealed around the corner. It transpires that existence is not a picture constructed by the soul but that which changes the soul. I have changed permanently after parting from you. I fled the past which, though it was an incomplete act of some play, haunts me as the curtain descends on the stage and I'm sitting in an empty auditorium on a broken chair. This is due to an abrupt precipice in our relations as far as I am concerned. The inability of us to reach accord about how 'we' can be. I cannot ultimately comprehend why this is so. However, thinking is also beyond our control and we do not ultimately understand why we think this or that thing anyway.

The reply came one week later. Yulia wrote that he was important to her as a man and it was hard for her not to be in touch with him. She wanted to talk to him. He had received the message one week before he touched down in Kyiv.

Chapter Fifteen

The military council of the field commanders of the DPR and LPR have authorised me to make the following announcement, which I request you to distribute as far as possible. The council will meet before the end of the month. This meeting must determine the question of creating a Ministry of Defence for Novorossiya. The idea of a MoD is supported by 90% of the LPR field commanders and a majority of the DPR field commanders. They support the creation of a MoD and the establishment of an integrated Novorossiya, rather than the separate DPR and LPR. The idea is also supported by the Cossacks. It is clear, however, that the leadership of the DPR and LPR opposes the creation of a single Novorossiya army. The majority of field commanders are ready to fight to the end for the creation of Novorossiya as a state. They will not retreat because Russia is behind them.

From an item on the infoodessa.com site, 23.09.2014

At half past nine Sergei left the hotel and headed for the metro. A few stations and a two hundred metre walk later he was at the spot where they had arranged to meet. Fresh morning air wafted over the verandah of the spacious café where he sat. The coolness of dawn had not yet had time to dissipate into the hot, stuffy air rising above grey, stone buildings. The impression was created that all left-bank Kyiv comprised carelessly strewn flat domino pieces, which had somehow landed perpendicular to the ground high above into the dense greenery of the city and they had scuffed up pillars of dust. The dust, when it settled, had congealed into roads, pavements, fences, and the rectangles of small shops and kiosks. It particularly seemed like this if viewed from the area on the hills of the right bank. Sergei sat in one of the outlying buildings and observed how he was overhung by the grey planes of hundreds of residential blocks that seemed ready to tumble atop one another and ruin all the left bank.

At two minutes to ten, wearing grey trousers and a white blouse, she burst through the drowsy realm of lacquered tables, white metal chairs and the tired visages of the waiters.

"Hi," she said, smiling and arranging her hair.

"Hello Yulia," replied Sergei, slowly looking her up and down.

They sat for half a minute, just looking at each other, before a waiter appeared and broke the silence.

"Coffee without sugar," Yulia requested. Smiling at Sergei again, she asked, "How's your life going, is there any news of your brother?"

"He's at the front, I think he's realising himself through the war. Any kind of life is a canvas for him and he paints his story against a backdrop of bombings and murders," Sergei replied.

"He's competing with you and showing that he can do something too, demonstrating, through his actions, that he is a man who can realise himself and find his place in life," she responded.

Sergei hesitated. He yearned to say he did not have enough conversations with her and receive her opinion, which he valued, often enough, but he could not say it aloud. He also wanted to know why she needed to meet him. Perhaps she had changed her mind and, even better, broken up with her husband and could now have a relationship with Sergei.

He did not have long to wait. Yulia pushed back her hair, looked at him abashed and blurted out, "I'm pregnant!"

The phrase rang around Sergei's ears for a few seconds. He stared at her. "Pregnant? How? You're messing with me?" he almost yelled. Then he twitched in his seat, stared at her face and thought she would start laughing.

But no, her cold, sculptural visage was frozen into a mask of indifference. She looked at Sergei, who was trembling at her news. He jumped up, sat, rose again, walked around the table, sat, looked at Yulia and covered his face with his hands. She looked at him coldly, as if trying to peer deep into his spirit and see his pain. She looked at him not as an accomplice in his suffering but as a detached bystander. Sergei moaned so loudly that the waiter stared at him from behind the bar.

"But how is it possible? Kolia is clearly sterile," he shouted and stopped, collapsing on to the table.

"I'm shocked myself, I don't understand how it happened," she said, icily watching her ex-lover writhe uncomfortably.

This was the turn of events Sergei had least expected. A volcano erupted inside him. He examined her body, as if trying to find an indication that she was lying. However, Yulia sat in silence, gazing stonily and unflinchingly into his eyes. "Is it possible? I said come to me," Sergei sighed.

The waiter came with a coffee and looked suspiciously at him. The estranged couple sat for half a minute, not knowing where to look.

"How's Kolia? Is he happy?"

"He's happy. Probably," she replied.

"What now? You're always complaining, like an overworked horse, that your inner pain won't allow you to be successful," Sergei said.

"Probably, only I have somehow lived these past three years," she replied. Tears trickled from her eyes. "I don't know why, it's as if there were something living inside me. Some small, frightened animal. It tears at me from within. I have concealed it far within myself but it's always trying to escape."

Sergei looked at Yulia's stony face where tears furrowed her cheeks, her mouth and her chin, like a vein glittering on a marble slab. He wanted to say that everything would be okay and to hold her close to him. However, he did not even dare to stretch his hand towards her, his whole body shook as if electrocuted, and the tremors surged in waves through his spirit. A few minutes passed. They looked at each other. There was a sense that the space around them swarmed with electrically charged words, like atoms colliding and dispersing chaotically. It seemed that the half metre between them was full of phrases, admissions and regrets. If only one of them had spoken, the second would have caught their words and they both would have shed tears in unison. But neither dared to speak a word.

"I wish you luck in your new life. Let it be a healthy baby," Sergei said slowly, as if every word were a cartridge in a magazine, mechanically reaching his lips.

"Thanks," said Yulia, gloomily.

The waiter came to see if they needed anything, but noting the sombre faces and receiving no reply he backed off.

"I can't ever communicate with you again."

"I understand."

"Even if I write to you, please do not reply. Please save me from myself," he said, looking at her pleadingly.

She wanted to say that yes they would not see each other again but could not. She just managed to nod.

Sergei's world had collapsed within an hour. He still hoped that Yulia could become his wife, even if it was in some far future. He thought that although she had not accepted his proposal now, her heart would soften, but as he looked at the icy face of the woman he loved he knew this was their last meeting. "I'm going," he said, and without waiting for an answer he darted into the street.

Clouds blanketed the sky and it grew cold. As he walked he shivered, not knowing whether it was an atmospheric or spiritual cold that affected him. He quickened his pace as he swerved around passersby, noticing neither their faces nor his surroundings. His legs carried him to the metro. His hand automatically pushed a token in the slot at the barrier and he ascended to the platform. He merged into the column of passengers and watched people entering and exiting the carriages. The train was like a wondrous serpent, devouring and disgorging them without distinction as to whom it absorbed and released. Its actions did not halt the flow of life itself. The doors rattled open and closed, the trains arrived and departed, people pushed their way hither and thither. Tears gathered in the corners of Sergei's eyes, almost ready to fall, just a little more moisture was required and they would trickle into liberty.

Chapter Sixteen

The Ataman of the Russian Cossacks in Antratsyt is also preparing to advance on Kyiv. "The lands of what is now East Ukraine belong historically to the Great Army of the Don Republic," was the announcement made by the commander of the 'so called' National Guard of the Great Army of the Don Republic, a Russian citizen named Nikolai Kozitsyn. "It has been legally established that the land as far as, and inclusive of, Kharkiv belongs to the Don army. The Cossacks lived on this land, which is now under occupation, for hundreds of years," Kozitsyn stated, "our next stop is Kyiv." We note that Kozitsyn and his militants currently occupy Antratsyt. The other towns under the control of the Cossacks are Krasnyi Luch, Rovenky, Perevalsk, Pervomaisk and Stakhanov. Alchevsk, according to Kozitsyn, is also under their control.

From an item on the NBN site, 09.10.2014

At five in the morning, a group of militia moved along the approaches to the airport, together with fresh forces from the Russian military, comprising four hundred troops in total. A number of trucks halted on the approach to the old terminal. Troops dressed in light-brown camouflage jumped from under the cloth covering the trucks and dispersed slowly in different directions. They had decided to attack from various areas of the airport. Artist was in the first wave. They would draw fire from the defenders while the other attackers moved in from the flanks. Three dozen of the troops gathered at the corner of a single-storey building, which gave a view of the location of the Ukrainian forces. The young man Artist had noted on the previous evening was among their number. He stared forwards, as if wanting to peer within the ragged fissures of the ruined terminal held by the foe.

Artist turned to him and asked, "What's in there, can

we see anything?"

"They're hiding and we'll smoke them out. Our reconnaissance says they have no armoured vehicles, they were recently pulled out," the young militant replied confidently.

Artist wanted to say that this was too presumptuous, but Motorola butted in. He said that in a couple of minutes Grad and Uragan artillery located in Makiivka would bombard the airport. After the artillery barrage, the reconnaissance forces would move in. After had he finished speaking they heard the distinctive fizzing sound of Grad missiles launching, and soon the other artillery joined the chorus. The thunder of the exploding missiles shook the terminal building. It was as if the earth's crust beneath them had broken clamorously in two. There was five minutes of infernal deafening noise. Artist's mind filed with images of the bloodied corpses of the Ukropi, some with severed limbs. They twisted in the agonies of death. All that was required now was to go in and finish them off. A group of tanks roared nearby. The first two vehicles would accompany Artist's unit. They were attacking the enemy straight from the front.

"C'mon motherfuckers, get the ball rolling," Motorola screamed, pushing fighters towards the corner that faced the terminal.

The first three militiamen ducked and darted into the area before the Ukrainians' positions. Artist dashed around the corner with the second group, firing a few rounds from his AK towards the enemy. The gunshots soothed the soul of this inhabitant of Rovenky. He advanced hurriedly alongside one of the tanks; its carcass lumbered over the ground, as if dissatisfied with being woken at the crack of dawn, and moved slowly in its sleepiness. Artist kept close to its armoured hulk, shooting occasionally and trying to see the Ukrainian soldiers. A young man was running towards the terminal nearby. As the building they had set off from receded, they emerged into an empty area of the airport and saw the twisted remains of the new terminal.

Its scorched and dilapidated carcass resembled the backdrop to a post-apocalyptic film. The broken windows were like an old man's toothless jawbone among the crumpled panels and naked skeletal frames. The ladder by the arrival terminal's docking station was bullet riddled and torn.

The tank fired at the front of the terminal and the boom was followed by the chime of shattering glass and a wall of smoke. Artist moved slightly to the side. In front of him a dark recess, the crater left by shelling, gaped and he needed to get around it. After he took a few steps he was suddenly flung to one side by an explosion. The Ukrainians were firing directly at the tank, probably with a powerful anti-tank weapon. The vehicle's turret was flung into the air by the blast. It hovered between the sky and the earth for a second, then assumed a slight angle and fell, covering the young man. The air itself broke apart from the sound of explosions and firing. The death cry of the militiaman and the noise of his bones cracking under the turret were dissolved within an inconceivable engulfing sound. Artist fell, slumped face-down on the ground for a moment. He raised his head to see what was happening. A burning man climbed out of the gaping aperture in the tank where the turret had been. His sickening scream filled the airfield. While the air engulfed his cries, the next wave of militants advanced and occasionally fired their automatic weapons. A second explosion sounded. The other tank, which had covered their advance, was now ablaze. A heavy stream of fire poured from the terminal. Artist rolled into the crater and all he could hear was the whistle of bullets, which persisted unceasingly for five minutes. Mortars boomed, their shells raking the attacking militiamen on the open area before the terminal. They were lined up like targets in a shooting range. Artist tried to raise his head above the crater, but a sniper's bullet nearly did for him and raised a small cloud of brown dust nearby. He pressed closer to the ground. Stalemate. He could not climb out of the crater, but he was still a danger to the enemy. The exploding mortars reminded him of a woman's footsteps as she approached with a scythe.

The shooting subsided but rose again with overwhelming waves of sound. Two more tanks had advanced to help the militants, along with an armoured vehicle and a truck with anti-aircraft guns. The fire from these quashed the Ukrainian snipers. Several troops rose from the ground and, crouching, headed for the approaching armoured vehicles. Artist could have joined them but decided to linger in his crater. The troops reached the tank and hid behind its armour.

"Well, it's time, as they say, to show that I'm a real man," said Artist, raising himself.

Suddenly, there was a powerful explosion, swiftly followed by another equally powerful blast; and then a third. He threw himself into the crater. Chunks of earth, dust, and even fragments of clothing showered on his head. The Ukrainian artillery was shelling them with Howitzers located in the nearby village of Pisky. The tanks blazed like ignited paper. In the overpowering roar few noticed how the Ukrainian snipers took out the more careless militiamen. The more experienced among them had flopped on to the ground and rolled into a crater or taken cover behind the scorched remnants of armoured vehicles. There was a minute's interval before the Howitzers boomed again. The armoured vehicle turned back and roared away swiftly towards the refuge of the one-storey building. The truck with the anti-aircraft guns attempted to reverse, but a direct hit flipped both its cabin and gun around.

The first wave of attack had been drowned in blood and it was unclear how many had survived. Time dilated and it seemed as if Artist had been lain in the crater for a whole day. In reality only one hour had passed. The longer he lay there, the more he tried to be conscious of this moment, the automatic in his hands, the dirty camouflage fatigues, and his position in the open expanse of the airport strewn with corpses. *How could he capture the moment wherein he was transfixed like some ancient insect within a drop of amber? Where was he located now on the linear trajectory of life?*

At eleven o'clock the characteristic hum of approaching tanks became audible as the second wave of attack approached. Artist sighed with relief. He turned his head and counted six tanks. They lumbered forward slowly, like vast dark tortoises, over the desiccated ground of the airport. Approximately one hundred soldiers scurried alongside the humming armoured vehicles. A stream of fire poured from the terminal, like drops sprayed from a shower head. The shooting intensified and the tanks replied with the occasional volley of shells. The men lying on the ground slowly crept towards the terminal to link up with those who had preceded them. Artist similarly stretched out on the ground and started to snake away from the crater, but then changed his mind and writhed back. He would wait for the reinforcements to get closer.

The building defended by the Ukrainian troops seemed to be coming apart at the seams. The sound of shattering glass formed an invisible wall in front of its façade. The second attack was larger and more effective than the first wave. If the pressure was sustained, the militia would be able to draw as close as possible to the building and then take it by storm.

Artist tensed. The line of attacking soldiers was approaching and he needed to join them. He heard the roar of attack engines and the calls of the militants to his rear. Then something incredible happened. When the nearest tank was thirty metres away, a short and piercing whistle was heard. It was followed by a rumble that shook the earth. The Ukrainian air force was attacking with high precision missiles. They fired from a distance without entering the airspace above the battle zone. The pilots targeted the tanks and the groups of militants. The screams of wounded soldiers mingled with the explosions, the racket of shrapnel and whistle of missiles. They formed a cloud of sounds covering the field. A crater was blasted open near the first tank, due to an inaccurate missile, but the next projectile was right on target. The tank flipped a little sideways and flopped partially into a crater where some soldiers were ensconced. It crushed them instantly. Artist looked out once and saw the metal torso of the tank weighing down on their bodies. Two demented voices wailed, adding to the cacophony of battle. He had no way out. Going back meant certain death.

Artist crawled to the terminal where he had seen the remains of an observation booth behind which he might hide. As he approached, he suddenly saw a dugout excavated by Ukrainian volunteers. He rolled into it. Aircraft continued to 'iron out' the open area behind him and fire streamed from the terminal in reply. Artist later found out that all the militia's armoured vehicles had been hit. The cries of wounded men filled the air, but no one could reach them. Over one hundred corpses were strewn over the battlefield. After fifteen more minutes had passed, silence fell abruptly; its advent was so sudden that his ears rang. Artist lay in the dugout and counted off all the saints he knew. He spoke to a higher presence which hovered above this earthly hell. He asked for help, like a child asks its parents for help with the pain after it has hurt itself. He sat up and peered out of the dugout. The battlefield resembled a scene from a war film; twisted bodies, burning tanks and severed limbs were like the backdrop to an epic set on the eastern front. His radio squealed. He had forgotten about it.

"Calling base, are you receiving, Artist?" he said dully leaning back against the wall of the dugout. There was only white noise in response. No one replied. After a few minutes he repeated his call. The radio crackled into life.

"It's Motorola, how are you Artist, are you wounded?"

He breathed a sigh of relief, all was not lost, he might get out somehow. "What should I do? There are a lot of wounded on the field," he reported.

"The hell with them, we can't help, even if we wanted to," said Motorola before pouring out a stream of every foul expletive he knew at the Ukropi.

But really who were these Ukropi and why did they put up such fierce defence? If their fascist ideology contained such hate for the inhabitants of Donbas, why were they fighting and dying here? Was it not suicide? Holding on to the airport for so many months, holding out in a half-ruined building and living while continuously under fire. Were they so brainwashed that they were ready to become suicidal warriors in the name of the 'Kyiv Junta'? Artist reflected and could not find a logical response to the question of the identity of his enemy or what moved them to wish his destruction.

At one o'clock in the afternoon he heard the roar of approaching tanks. The Russian military had arrived with almost three dozen, newly modernised T 72 tanks. Russian paratroopers were their advance guard. They dispersed into their individual positions and approached the terminal. They unleashed all their weapons against the airport buildings. The paratroopers had reached the old terminal when Ukrainian Grad and Uragan missiles showered down on them, but this did not halt the attack. Russian troops occupied the old terminal building and the adjoining hotel and garage. They strengthened their position and continued moving towards the new terminal not far from the dugout where Artist lay. Russian tanks remorselessly approached and shelled the building. There were so many troops and armoured vehicles it seemed like the battle of the Kursk Salient. This was a turning point in the skirmish.

Artist looked around and the tanks were gasping not far behind him. However, as the second Ukrainian Air Force commenced its bombardment, the racket, which could tear the eardrum, was concentrated in one place, at one point. Even the sound of one of these explosions alone seemed enough to flip a person inside out. Some tanks turned to the right and away from the terminal, a couple were ablaze, but some still advanced.

Artist ran a few steps and joined the advancing paratroopers. Almost all the armoured vehicles remained to the rear, but a couple of Russian tanks were providing cover through the crannies between the concrete plates to the front of the terminal. In front of him a paratrooper fired through a shell hole in the building, preventing the Ukrainians from firing back through it.

A large group, supported by the tank shelling, penetrated the first floor of the new terminal. Artist was only fifty metres away from the building. He darted onwards, stooped, then ran forward, attacking randomly. The Ukrainian military fired the odd round close to him, but the trajectory of the bullets somehow shifted a little to the side of his course. He reached a gaping hole in the building, which was crammed with fragments of concrete, missiles and glass, and pressed against the adjacent wall. He dared not peer inside the structure. He now had a view of the battlefield in front of the terminal. The picture pierced his imagination: he saw the smoke from shattered tanks penetrated the sky in heavy, dark furls of fabric and the twisted carcasses of trucks, between which T 72s weaved and soldiers darted forwards. Someone dropped like a tin can in a firing range; here and there a shell fired by the Ukrainian Howitzers in Pisky exploded.

Artist bowed his head and looked into the hole in the wall near him. He shunted his way cautiously forward through the debris. Inside, the floor was littered with broken glass and there was a barricade of chairs reinforced with sandbags, and beyond that a shop; its products were scattered along the floor, together with fragments of the ceiling. Smoke belched from the next aperture in the wall to his left. It was unclear what was going on there. He heard shooting. It was simply hell. The paratroopers penetrated the opening, one man at a time, covering each other. Then they were sprayed with machine gun fire from the second floor and the interior barricades. Here and there they managed to advance and strengthen their positions.

Artist rushed to take cover behind a fragment from a fallen concrete block. He was relatively safe for a few seconds. He raised his automatic and fired a few rounds at the second floor. A second later he looked around the block to inspect his situation. That took only three seconds, just three seconds, but the picture that presented itself before him seemed to stretch through time. There was an opening in the sandbag barricade inside the building. Someone had been felled by the blast from a grenade launcher and some of the sacks were pushed aside to create a passage. Two paratroopers rushed towards the opening, trying to make it to the centre of the building, but a Ukrainian soldier lay in the torn, shredded aperture in the barrier. The explosion from a grenade had wounded him and he was motionless, as if dead. The first paratrooper ran to the gap in the barricade and fired through it. The second approached from the direction of the concrete block concealing Artist. Then a third joined them to provide cover fire. Artist was still looking when the explosion happened. Three seconds. The Ukrainian volunteer had blown himself up, along with the three paratroopers, without any cries of Slava Ukraiini or anything similar. Perhaps he could have stayed alive and been captured, but he had chosen to sacrifice himself. The blast wave, mixed with blood, shook the concrete around him. Artist ducked instinctively. Plaster and fragments of sandbags showered him. A bloodied hand flopped to the ground nearby.

During just a few months of war Artist had seen so much: intestines, human entrails, blood, and a severed head, but he had never seen someone sacrifice their life like that. *For what? Is it possible that having a chance to live you would opt to blow yourself apart? What sense was there in it, what were the last thoughts flickering through the Ukrainian volunteer's mind? Was it perhaps an ideal, something stronger than the fear of death or desire for a future? Or the thirst for revenge? What?*

While the smoke rose to the middle of the first floor, Artist rushed from the building, gulping down the fresh air. Suddenly he felt a fatal sense of fatigue. Today had squeezed him dry. He wanted to flee somewhere where he would not hear shots and explosions.

"Artist, respond," the radio squealed with Motorola's voice.

"I am in the terminal," he muttered in reply.

"Run back to where I am, motherfucker," the commander ordered.

A minute later Artist was crossing the battlefield to the militants' base. The Russian military had managed to hold their position on the ground floor of the terminal, but the exchange of fire in the building continued.

Artist occasionally ran or sometimes just accelerated his stride. He wove between crumpled tanks and mutilated corpses. Black volcanic-like smoke rose over the old terminal. The building was on fire and would probably not be standing much longer. Ash and the stench of corpses hung in the air. He halted by one of the corpses for a few minutes. It was the body of a militiaman lain in the short, yellowed grass. One leg was torn off, as if someone had pulled at it for a long time. Slivers of flesh hung from its carbonised edges, along with dark, seared blood. The right arm was twisted unnaturally. In the middle of the abdomen, through the damaged armoured vest, was a brown, gaping wound. The soldier's helmet had slipped down and obscured most of his face, but some familiar features were recognisable. Artist lifted the helmet with the barrel of his AK. It was the corpse of Chervonets lying before him. His lifeless, cloudy eyes seemed full of the fear of death and its frightening emptiness. As if there were nothing beyond the boundaries of human life; and this was the more terrifying aspect of the corpse. Chervonets's face was a frozen mask of perplexity and surprise at the encounter with a vacuum outside of life itself. *Was there a void there or just more torment?* The dead man's eyes seemed to express the horror of realising his death. The moment of cognition of the absence of space beyond the boundaries of existence. Everything was engulfed by that fear. The battle, the rumbling of war itself, the past, parents, family. Those eyes were now filled with dead and terrifying mirrors, as if in the last moment Chervonets had been conscious that he would never reach the broken windows of the Pentagon.

Artist continued on his path and soon reached the auxiliary building near the old terminal. Beneath its wall, which protected them from stray shots, over a dozen wounded men lay. A field nurse scurried from one to the next. There was a heap of corpses a little further away. They would be removed at some point. A number of soldiers peered around a concrete block towards the terminal. Motorola was sitting on the steps of the building with a couple of soldiers by him. They were pointing at a plan of the underground utilities network at the airport, indicating its access points and lay out. He nodded his head in support of what they were saying.

"Artist, come here," Motorola summoned him. The commander looked at Artist with exhausted eyes. His red beard hung in straggling wisps and he tried to pull fragments of debris from it with his fingers. Motorola seemed not only tired but as tense as a high pitched string. All his hatred towards his past life was concentrated on the possibility of a military defeat which might now be realised. His whole appearance showed that this war was something personal for him. That which is concealed in the heart grows there and will bear fruit one day. Losing here and now meant a return to his past life. It meant becoming nothing, being lowered below the pedestal on which he now stood. He trembled from malice and his impotent inability to change anything. He could barely restrain himself. He screamed

146

for no reason and swore at anyone nearby. He needed a triumph like a heart needed blood. This was his life. He summoned Artist and told him what they were planning.

It transpired that below the new terminal there was a small network of old catacombs, which had not been removed when the facility was constructed. They had, on the contrary, been reinforced, creating a kind of corridor. This passage extended some distance into the area where the battle had just taken place. There were two exits that reached the surface of the battlefield and these were clearly indicated in the plan he was examining. According to their reconnaissance, the Ukrainian soldiers had concealed themselves there when the building was fired on with missiles.

"They are there now. I feel it with my heart. We'll fucking burn them out; if the flames don't work, the smoke will do it," he said, tapping the paper spread before him.

"It needs to be checked," a militiaman who was standing nearby suggested. His nickname was Crooked. His nose was a little out of kilter because he had taken up boxing as a teenager, clearly without much success.

"Never! The boys have squeezed the Ukropi into there. We need to help 'em. Look," Motorola said, nodding at Crooked, "say a vehicle with a fuel tank was driven there and if you laid explosives here and here, the explosion would expose the entrance to the catacombs. Then we'll just flood it with fuel and that'll be the end of 'em." Motorola slapped his hand on the plan.

Sappers were hurrying on to the battlefield a couple of minutes later. A fuel wagon followed behind them. Artist was sitting in its cockpit when the first explosion thundered. A second followed. Shots echoed from the terminal. The battle had not ceased there. The vehicle pulled up to the crater left by the first explosion and Artist jumped out and helped unreel the hose. When the petrol was flowing into the dark space of the catacomb, Artist noticed that the shooting ceased. The dark fuel streamed into the crater and all around there was silence except for occasional, distant gunshots. After five minutes, bullets whistled over his head again. It was clear that reinforcements had come and the Ukrainian snipers were at work. If was often impossible to work out where they were shooting from. The empty fuel tanker headed towards a building at the other side of the airport. A couple of people were preparing a torch to ignite the fuel.

"Motorola, it's weirdly quiet. Perhaps we should work out what's wrong," Artist spoke to his commander over the radio.

"Fuck you, you bastard, you don't get it," the commander shrieked in reply, and spewed out invectives. After a minute his stock of foul vocabulary was exhausted and Motorola said in a calmer voice, "I told you to burn them, burn them till nothing remains."

Artist clicked off the radio and grumbled irritably. Motorola never participated directly in the action. After Igor Girkin (Strelkov) had been deposed as head of the DPR and the militant Babai had been exposed as a mundane coward and fled to Crimea, only Motorola remained as a symbol. He embodied the image of resistance to the Ukrainian military, so he had not been seen on the battlefield for a long time. It was said that safeguarding him was a direct order from the Kremlin, but now it was necessary for him to deal with the situation personally and perhaps even appear on the battlefield, instead he just continued to bark out orders.

"Light it," cried Crooked cinematically, and threw the blazing torch into the crater.

The fumes and volume of the fuel combined with the narrowness of the passage generated a small explosion. Flames, seemingly as unreal as a special effect, streamed upwards in a slender pillar. Another pillar of fire streamed out from the other entrance to the catacombs. The soldiers scurried from the scene. After three minutes, when they returned to their unit's position, they were met by a pallid Motorola, who was sitting, as before, on the steps. All the blood had drained from his face and it was as pale as a newly laundered white sheet. When asked what had happened, he just switched on the radio. The wavelength used by the Russian military rang with the screams of men, like burning sinners in hell, trying to ease their pain. It transpired that when the militiamen had blown up the entrances, the Ukrainians had attacked the Russian paratroopers and compelled them to retreat into the catacombs and await help. That was the moment the firing had ceased, just when Motorola had given the order to ignite the fuel.

The demented inhuman cries echoed from the radio, tearing the air around the red-bearded car thief. A dozen or so militia stood beside him. A cold breeze wafted over them. After a minute everything went quiet. To the left of the commander an autumn leaf, yellowed by the season, fell and circled slowly, as if swirled by an unseen hand. Artist looked at Motorola, paralysed by not knowing what to do. The commander wandered over the grass as if drunk, stumbled over the tussocks and clutched at stunted trees. He seemed to need to put in a lot of effort just to keep his balance. Then suddenly he screamed like a wounded fighter on the battlefield. But no one hurried to help him.

A carnival of phases swirled through Artist's head. He sympathised with his commander, but began to despise him for his unjustifiable cruelty and inhumanity. Thoughts crept through his mind like lines of text drifting up a computer screen. *What was it for, all this death, where was that ideal for which they were fighting? He did not find an answer to any of these questions.*

Three days later Artist asked that he be allowed to return to his camp near Luhansk. As he was leaving the airport he saw two truckloads of soldiers arriving to replace the slain men.

He returned to the Luhansk camp late at night. He rose next morning, exited his tent, walked through the base and headed for the *Zelentsi*, or green area, a small forest clearing bristling with growth. Some bird darted between the branches. The wind fluttered, as if caught in heaped leaves, twitching like a human soul. The sun gently stroked his face and he lifted his head and closed his eyes, spending a minute soaking up the sunshine. When he opened his eyes there was a shrill whistle. A splash like a stone in water. His legs buckled as he reached towards his right shoulder. A bright red blot bloomed on his arm. Blood dripped from his fingers on to the earth and the ragged tufts of withered, almost golden, grass.

Chapter Seventeen

The illegal consumption of gas by the DPR and LPR will lead to losses of UAH 7bn for Ukraine.

The uncontrolled and unpaid consumption of gas on the territory of Donbas, under militia control, will lead to Ukraine losing UAH 7bn (approximately USD 538m) by the end of the year, according to the chair of Naftogaz Ukraiiny, Serhiy Perelom. "In September, this area consumed almost 27 million cubic metres of gas, and in October its consumption will be approximately 100 million cubic metres. This means that in October alone, the gas, which was purchased by the company via reverse flow and donated to cover the requirements of this territory, will mean losses of UAH 700m (approximately USD 53m) for Naftogaz. There is no limit to the potential cost to Naftogaz before the end of the year, but it could be a figure of up to UAH 6-7bn," Perelom stated.

A news article on the Unian news agency site, 31.10.2014

Anatolii Nedelkov, Sergei's and Anton's father, awoke with a head that felt like concrete. If he moved it in any direction, agony reverberated through his brain. He counted to ten while looking at the ceiling, like he usually did while gathering the strength to visit the bathroom. He stretched his hand to the telephone and saw there were dozens of missed calls and messages. Something had happened but an aversion to life overruled his desire to know exactly what had occurred. He had drunk far too much again yesterday, and his wife, Irina, had hidden at their neighbours' place. He almost always drank to the point of oblivion. His unhealthy relationship with alcohol had begun in 1975 when he graduated from Rostov College of Art.

Anatolii's friends called him Tolik, known affectionately

as Toliasha by his father; he had begun painting on the walls of their home when he was five years old. His mother thrashed the curly haired toddler, who did not understand that he had done anything wrong, but his father had seen something unusual in the boy. Eventually, Toliasha studied at the specialty arts school in Rovenky before enrolling in the Rostov College of Art.

He was once waking by the river in Rostov while looking at the aluminium sharpness of the water; its surface was rumpled with the narrow folds of the waves and a silver light, and he could not look enough. In the arid Steppe of the Donbas area he was accustomed only to seeing the small bulge of occasional hills and the murky, uneven distance pyramided with slag heaps. His eyes were accustomed to the abrasiveness of that dry space. There was only a small, slender stream in the village where he had lived, which ran through the gardens and fell into a pond with a ragged bank.

When Tolik was fourteen he had ventured far into the Steppe, where ragged solitary clumps of dog-rose towered over the grass seared by the summer sunshine. He took off his light, checked shirt, stripped to his waist, and ran swiftly on to a mound; he stretched out his arms instinctively, like wings. Then he ran over the desiccated black earth, which was mazed with the cracks. These dark recesses, similar to the lines of a vast cobweb, swathed the entire field. The pale-blue sky above had not shed rain for a long time, so the web had grown and intertwined in fantastic knots. Tolik ran ahead and strength surged through him. He understood that the wind drove the evil spirits of mundanity, teenage angst and sorrow from him. He rose up the hill like the ship borne on the ninth wave in the famous painting, then swooped like a bird down the other side of the hillock.

In Rostov, he had become overcome by feelings he did not understand as he stood at the edge of an observation dock by the river. The water splashed as softly as a lullaby, as if

152

murmuring something to him of its aqueous self, imperceptible to the locals. Those who are accustomed to hearing its rustling and sighs do not know of what the river speaks. Tolik listened to the murmur of the waves, which stretched out before him, as if bowing and shattering, and saw how they levelled out before striking the stone jetty.

He began coming to the river every day and listening to its soft moan. After several long months his thirst for this enticing moistness was still not assuaged. It gathered in his soul like in a sponge. He received, but did not give, he poured the river's riches into himself, but was not eroded. The river changed him as an artist. From that time his paintings were filed with colour saturated with the spectrum, awash with many hues. Tolik realised how to imbue the picture with a soul, to crucify it on to the canvas and to merge it with the landscape into a single whole.

That same evening he returned to the room he rented in an old woman's house, he felt invigorated and lay down to sleep. He saw images in his mind of the Steppe, not arid as it usually appeared but pierced by streams that led to a fantastic river; the river eroded the banks with its tensile flow, bending like a competing gymnast around its swerving course. This was the world of his soul, its slender delicate tissue, vulnerable but also supple and plastic. After a few days he executed a painting and took it to his lecturer, Albert Moiseevich Kaminskyi.

"Albert Moiseevich, I want to show you something. In my opinion it isn't too bad," he said to his teacher, who was sitting in an otherwise empty classroom.

Tolik raised the picture. The deep, powerful river flowed through the Donbas Steppe where it could not exist in reality. Small green shoots sprouted on its banks. The right side was fecund with the image of a slag heap that hung over the water like a black unearthly rock. It was another land, another Donbas brimming to its limits with flowing, life-giving water.

"You know this is something unusual Anatolii. The palette is of course bright and exaggerated, there is a lot of expressiveness, but on the whole…" The lecturer stroked his professorial beard as he looked at the canvas in some astonishment. Anatolii showed him his newest works on a few subsequent occasions. His lecturer would look at the student then the canvas and smile at something only he comprehended. Tolik never knew what Albert Moiseevich was thinking as he looked enigmatically at the undersized, skinny man from a provincial town, whose existence he had never suspected. This young man from that obscure place amazed him with his brush strokes, the movement of light in his canvases and their translucent shadows.

They soon proposed organising Tolik's first exhibition, albeit in the corridor of the college. However, for a young, rural man this was more significant than any previous recognition of his ability. He always remembered how he had passed by the walls and looked at his pictures as if at a stranger's. Simultaneously, he felt the impulses that had engendered them in his breast. It was his soul hanging on the walls. He was like a guard dog strolling through the college and protecting his ego. He even brought his mother, Zoia Fedorovna Shevchenko, from the village. She was a plump woman who wore a simple dress and a headscarf. She walked from one picture to the next, unable to understand where her son had acquired his gift and how such a talented and sensitive man had emerged in their family.

The event horizon of the pictorial arts opened ahead of Tolik. Albert Moiseevich approached him while he was on the last module of his course, "You know, Anatolii, I have certainly lived a lot in my time, I have seen a lot and am well experienced, as they say."

"People begin talking like that when they are going to say something important," said Tolik.

"Important? Yes, yes, this is especially important.

Somehow, during the course of fate, by ways unknown to me, you have, in the past three years, travelled the road which took me thirty years to travel." The professor stroked his beard as he talked, "So we are aiming for you to undertake further studies and have recommended you to Leningrad University."

Tolik did not believe his ears. He wanted to hug his elderly teacher, to scream loudly and leap for joy. Albert Moiseevich looked carefully at his reaction, examining his face and eyes, as if trying to see something more than delight therein.

A week after the course and before the final exams had ended, he entered the Alenushka café, which was not far from the college. He often went there and sat near the window to look at the passers-by as they flickered past cinematically. It seemed to him that the crowd's motion resembled the bustle of atoms; they were chaotic, heading nowhere, without a trajectory, but they symbolised some internal sense of life. This random streaming contained the essence of things, and simultaneously this motion always led to some result. People stepped seemingly aimlessly, but obligatorily came to some goal. This multiply vectored, accidental movement was impossible to anticipate.

"Hey, is this place free?" asked a Georgian, who stood in front of him and broke off Tolik's train of thought.

Tolik looked around the café and saw that all the other tables were occupied. "Yes, it's free," he said nonchalantly.

"Great, thanks pal," he replied in his accented Russian. "Givi, Aliko, this guy says we can sit here," he said in the direction of a couple of other inhabitants of the Caucasus.

Tolik almost winced at this. It would be awkward to refuse, but he did not want to sit with three strangers.

"Hey pal, what's to be sad about? Let's drink to our meeting," said the first Georgian, who, it transpired, was named Gia.

Tolik knew his own weakness. During his first year at college he had gone to a classmate's birthday bash and got so drunk that he did not remember leaving. The day after the party he also had a lot of blanks.

"Not for me," he said seriously.

"Why is that, are you an athlete eh?" said Givi, smiling.

"No, I'm an artist," replied Tolik, not understanding the joke.

"Vakh's an artist; that's my uncle Vakhtang, he draws mountains, sheep, grapes; you want to kiss his pictures," said Gia.

Tolik just smiled. He had no real friends and loved solitude, reflecting on things and roaming the city with his thoughts. Now he wanted to breathe easily and rid himself of the stress in which he had lived over the past few months while giving his all to every canvas. But the newcomers would not leave him alone and were disrupting his plans.

"This is wine here, not piss, the real stuff from Kakheti. My uncle sent it. You'll thank me, honest son, go on," Gia said slowly.

He moved the side of his grey coat to reveal a bottle of some dark-red liquid.

"Okay, pour it out then," said Tolik, equally slowly, with a measure of fear in every word he spoke.

They drank first to their meeting and then for international friendship, then for Ukraine, Georgia, women, for the oldest among them, for their parents, for Tolik's studies in Leningrad. And that was it. Here the thread of events, wound on to a bobbin in Tolik's head, snapped. It seemed that in the next moment he was lying on a couch in an unfamiliar room with striped wallpaper. There was a table nearby, littered with wine bottles and plates smeared with the remnants of some dark-red stuff. His head was boiling like soup over a naked flame, bubbling and steaming. Tolik looked around and saw two men who were of Caucasian nationality, but could not for the life of him remember who they were.

"Gia, Gia, the artist is awake, look at what a state he's in," said one of the men and poured some red Saperavi wine from Georgia into a multi-faceted glass tumbler.

Things carried on like that for three weeks before Tolik somehow made it to college and found out he had missed his finals. He returned to the apartment and Gia.

"I've fucked up everything with my own hands," Tolik cried like a baby and thumped his fist on the table. He could not restrain the tears that were falling as thick as a hail shower down his face. He moaned like an injured dog and continued to pound the table with his fist again and again, and asked them to pour some more before gulping down another glass.

"That it should be so, because, get this, I could be great Givi, my paintings could be exhibited in the capital." He slurred as he sketched these castles in the air to his bosom buddy. The Georgians stared at him in silence. This soft, delicate, curly headed man sat on a chair with tears raining from him.

"Pal, you'll paint, you'll see," said one of the seated men.

"Why, why and for whom?" Tolik moaned explosively. "For whom will I paint?" he asked the other man, but no one could give him an answer.

Years passed but Tolik always remembered his state at that time; as if he were a home, the interior home of his spirit. The structure was burned out. He walked on the hearth, trying to find his familial possessions, the brushes, easel and paint. Everything was burned, charred and blackened. He wandered the ruins of his heart, touching the embers. He looked around and could not believe what had happened.

He was expelled from the college and a career as an artist was now inconceivable. He returned to Rovenky and got a job as a mechanical engineer at the mines. He simultaneously serviced the telephone lines of two adjacent villages. He was married one year later. His first son, Sergei, initially delighted him but subsequently troubled Tolik. His son's external appearance and his character were far removed from his own. However, Tolik loved his youngest boy as soon as he saw him at the hospital. The curly haired boy was no different from himself as a child. When he grew a little more he also painted brilliantly. Tolik regarded the youngster's artistic career as an extension of his own.

"Son, when you draw imagine that your spirit hovers in the air above the world, a city, a field. It should absorb the space and swell like a balloon. And, Son, the soul must, of necessity, explode. Everything that you take in must fly from you and unfurl across the picture," he said to little Anton

When the boy grew up and entered the institute, Tolik froze like a wounded bird every time he travelled to Luhansk to visit him; as if he were awaiting his own healing through his son. Unfortunately, the younger son was not able to defeat the Nedelkovs' familial curse; after that, life completely lost its meaning for his father.

On this particular morning another hangover was savaging him. Tolik pulled himself together and looked at the telephone. There were numerous messages all with the same text: *Anton has been shot*. He could not believe what he read and by the evening he was in the militia camp. As he passed by the heavy artillery, people here and there, and tents he prayed to heaven that Anton would live. When he reached the grey canvas tent where his son was lain Tolik froze as he had done once before his own paintings. Everything that was best in his life now lay before him. Anton alone gave his life some meaning. His son lay on a bed with closed eyes. *Had he died? How could that be?* Tears trickled down his face. He could not keep their streams and his sorrow locked inside.

Anton opened his eyes. "Dad, you came. You … you had to come…" Anton said before he fell into a semi-conscious state.

A Ukrainian sniper had been observing Artist when he

was standing by the bushes, but he had moved slightly and the bullet, which injured his lung, had already been removed. Tolik looked at his son, who was lain on an old bed with a chequered blanket covering his body. Anton's stubbled face was twisted in pain. His father drew closer, his hands frantically gripping his cloth carrier bag, and examined his child. Tears rolled down his face and his lips moved involuntarily as they muttered something. It seemed that no one could hear his quietly spoken words. Only a fly circled his head and heard his words.

Chapter Eighteen

In the towns in Luhansk Province, which have been liberated by the Ukrainian army, miners have begun to receive their back pay. The major focus of people in Ukraine at present is the east of the country. The problems of people in this region are snowballing: homes destroyed by the conflict, businesses closed down, empty shelves in shops and pharmacies, and increasing wage and pension arrears. The total sum of wage arrears in Donetsk Province increased by UAH 155m in one month, and by September amounted to UAH 310.523m. In Luhansk Province, total wage arrears increased by an even greater figure of UAH 161m, to UAH 242m. Judging by the way events are developing, debts in these regions will continue to increase.

From an item on the 'Fakty I Kommentarii' site, 28.10.2014

When Artist opened his eyes, the first thing that struck him was the silence. It hung in the air like an adhesive substance and stuck to everything nearby: the beds, chairs, some medications on the bedside table. After the explosion at the airport any silence seemed suspicious to him.

"Nurse, nurse, help," Artist's cry tore through the quietness.

A young woman rushed in with a bag of medication. "What's happened, is something hurting?" she asked.

"My shoulder is aching, it's twisting my arm," the sick man said, grimacing.

The nurse gave him an injection of local anaesthetic and a sedative. In his half-conscious state Artist picked up his tablet from the bedside table. A number of old, unread messages from Sergei glittered on the screen. His brother called on him to see sense. The self-proclaimed republic would not survive economically, a world built on war could not be ideal. It was enough to recollect how much blood the Soviet Union had been built upon and how that turned out. Sergei's letter concluded with a paragraph that Artist read, but barely understood it referred to him:

You know that I have always built my life upon mathematical principles. According to them, two times two is four, but with regard to life, it's five. Life is not logical. Elsewhere in Europe people do not care what is happening in Ukraine. But where you are in Donbas complete feudalism rules the people. Power belongs to the warlords. They are like princes and feudal lords. Political prospects are only enjoyed by those who can feed and provide for their 'unit'. It bears an absolute resemblance to the situation in Somalia, and in Chechnya in 1993-1994. You can be thrown into a vault within a couple of seconds or they can take away whatever they like from you. There is no popular rule. A disgusting state of affairs has developed; life in Novorossiya is not better than in Ukraine, but in fact far worse. It is literally hell, societal savagery, Sergei had written.

In his exasperation, Artist slammed the computer down. *What do you know? Were you ever, even once, in a battle? Have they threatened to kill you because you were an inhabitant of Donbas? We just want to live, but not with the 'Banderites'.* He thought irritably for a long time that there was no way back, that the people here could no longer live under the same roof as them. *One way or another this will be our country.*

"It's the one thing I live for now," Artist said finally, before slowly falling asleep.

Tolik came once more to his son and looked at him dozing. His younger son was so similar to him. Anton was still young and curls dangled lightly from his head. How brutally life had laughed at him, neither he nor his son could paint and live as they wished. Tolik sat on a chair and listened to the regular snorting breaths from the bed. It seemed as if he wanted to turn back time and return, in particular, to that day when he had talked to Albert Moiseevich. The lecturer had searched for something incomprehensible and elusive in Tolik. He now understood that Moiseevich had been searching for an indication of his resolve. That normal human firmness that helps to endure the hardship of creativity, the poverty of daily life, moral anguish and ulcerating doubt. He had sought for Tolik's desire to sacrifice himself to something higher and more attenuated, yet greater than daily life. With that quality it is possible to find the road which leads to spiritual realisation. Tolik had sought the path, winding imperceptibly through the grass, in everything; all the pictures and sketches that he had executed. However, the path consists of 'the self leading to the self'; as if its real essence were twofold. It was concealed, stolen by time and God knows what else. True, deep happiness and delight in life is possible only if you seek out your inner twin. Tolik now understood that neither he, his son, nor Albert Moiseevich had found that reality. This was various embodiments of a personal tragedy.

And how is Sergei, where is he now? He thought suddenly of his older son. He wanted to telephone him and talk to him, even about some neutral subject. Perhaps they could simply be silent, for silence occasionally unites people more than words. Hearing the breathing of another means that you can touch their spirit.

The battalion commander peered into the tent. "How is the soldier in here, is he getting better?" he asked, looking at the bed.

"So, where did he get to, to end up like this?" replied Tolik, then added, "and, come to think of it, how do I enrol in the militia?"

The battalion commander smiled. It sometimes happened that the relative of a dead or wounded soldier would replace them in the ranks. This war had long divided life in the occupied area of this region into two parts. One part was in the old Donbas; it always voted for the Party of the Regions, was mired in poverty and lived from paycheque to paycheque; its uniform existence stretched like dreary rubber over the years. The second part was the war, the explosions in cities, the bodies of relatives, and the military situation.

Only a few hours later Tolik was trying on a military uniform. There was no mirror nearby but he tried to look down his side to see how it fitted. The helmet pulled too much on his head, the jacket was tight around his stomach; even the boots that he could barely pull on, while grunting and swearing, looked unnatural. He was like a farmworker drafted into the army. Tolik strode up and down, shook his head and took the Kalashnikov he was given in his hands. An onlooker might have smiled at the appearance of such a soldier, however, anyone who had looked into Tolik's face at that moment would have changed their mind. A determined glint shone in his brown, tired and already aged eyes. His expression look like he was preparing to avenge himself, not on the Ukropi but on the whole world, for his personal failures, errors and miscalculations; as if Tolik's enemy were not now the Ukrainian army but life itself. Life was guilty of causing his broken and decrepit state. No one could help him now but himself. No one could stop him.

It took Tolik a long time to get to sleep that night. He tossed, turned, sighed and grunted. He was in a larger tent than where Anton was lain, next to snoring militiamen. Darkness embraced each of them, sliced by only a thin ray of moonlight which fell on to Nedelkov senior's blanket. He stretched out his hand. The moon-ray illuminated his palm, splintered and fell crookedly on the fibrous surface of his blanket. A few minutes passed like that. An old man, alone in his interior world, playing with glimmers of moonlight as if he sought in them some spectral, unearthly radiance of hope.

The following day a group of militiamen was dispatched to undertake a reconnaissance mission. Red-jowled fighters from a reconnaissance/sabotage unit bustled around the camp early in the morning. They were GRU, Russian Military Intelligence, Special Forces or Spetsnaz. They usually coordinated the action, especially if a deep penetration of enemy territory was required. However, today the Spetsnaz were occupied with a special task. They needed a local resident who would help their operation; drones had surveyed the area from above, but there was a blind spot in the green forested area near the town of Shchastia. The group's route passed by this location and so they needed someone to investigate the topographical features, but the Spetsnaz did not want to risk their own men.

Tolik rose early, as he always did, but this time it was the chatter of the men preparing for the day's task that had woken him. He exited his tent and saw the soldiers getting ready for the operation. They chatted happily and calmly, trading anecdotes and paying no heed to the old man. He wanted to pass through them but heard their conversation.

"Yes, shall we penetrate there, how do you see it?" a fair-haired and rosy-cheeked man asked his skinny partner. Both of them were smoking and checking their rifles.

"Eh, well there may be Ukropi there or there may not be. We don't want to be wasting our fire if not," the second one argued.

"If we sent someone in, they could go to the green area and check it and then the group can go further. What's eating you up?" The fair-haired man badgered his partner.

"Imagine one of us going in and after a kilometre the Ukropi sniffing him out," the other fighter insisted.

Anatolii butted into the conversation and said, "Lads, I can help you."

"You? You're an old man who just can't retire and live on his pension," chuckled the skinny man.

"What pension? Are you having a laugh? The Ukropi don't pay it out; they've wounded my son, I can't just sit on my hands," the old man said, justifying his presence.

His face expressed resolve for the first time in a long time. The two fighters fell silent and the pensioner talked and talked. "I fuckin' hate them with all my heart, I would grab them and cut them up like mad dogs," said Tolik. "Believe me, if I meet one of them on my way, I'll strangle him with my own hands." At this point Tolik was so engrossed in what he was saying that he moved forward to imitate the action of strangling someone. The two other men smiled and then, just in case, stepped back a little. "I have to do something, I can't just sit back and watch when my son is dying," Tolik said in a quieter voice.

The men looked disbelievingly at him and then at each other, then whispered together and decided to check it out with their commander. The question was swiftly resolved. One hour later Tolik was travelling over rough ground in a passenger car near to the line of their positions. Before they had travelled a couple of kilometres they exited the car and slowly distributed their weapons. Then they plunged into the green pelt of the roadside shrubbery. Moving along barely discernible trails, they reached the designated location. Nedelkov's task was simple; he had to comb through the territory under the guise of being a local resident who was checking out the plantation, then he simply had to return and report back.

"Come on Dad, don't let me down," said the fair-haired man.

Tolik grunted in response, and without looking around began heading towards the trees. He walked slowly for two hundred metres, looking over the vegetation and seemingly not thinking about anything. His heart pounded and his breathing was constricted. He was anxious. Each step took him near to the curling boughs and branches of the trees, and something pierced his breast at each step, but he was not frightened enough to turn and go back. On the contrary, something drew him to the designated spot. He walked unhurriedly, as if he was really just out for a walk, breathed the air and decided to look around. A bright, clear azure light poured from somewhere in the sky, streaking the greenery, which turned ultramarine and grew darker as it descended. A bird sang somewhere. The wind murmured in the leaves as if whispering to them of the countries where it had travelled. The wind had seen wild animals and birds and heard a speech composed of pure sound waves without meaning. Anatolii's life had become as empty of meaning as verbal gurgling, but he suddenly found himself staring at the lineaments of nature as if seeing them for the first time; as if he were not born in Donbas but had flown here from a distant corner of the world.

"This is great," uttered Tolik, astonished at the blissfulness of this morning. He thought at that moment the war would end and soon the guns would fall silent. He would return home with his son and they would both paint a picture. One large picture to encompass both of them; maybe a pacific landscape taken from the Donbas Steppe. This would be his life's work. He smiled suddenly and felt that before him was, as there should be, a future. Suddenly a deafening explosion sounded and black coils of smoke rose into the air.

That morning Sergei awoke with a heavy head. On the previous evening he had been drinking to attempt to alleviate his profound sorrow. A week had passed since he had learned that Yulia was pregnant. He had roamed the darkness of Kyiv for several nights, trying to blend in with passersby on its high and wide streets. He had come to the banks of the Dnipro and wandered its sands. He had entered the water until it touched his shins, barely restraining himself from being drowned. He had watched the water lapping his legs. His gaze was caught by

166

the waves cast up by motorboats as they hurtled past. Yesterday evening he had sat in an open area at a diner and had drunk far too much alcohol. He could not remember how he had made it back to his hotel room. This morning his head felt like it had been smashed in bits. He rose from the bed, groaned and clutched his temples. He managed to get up somehow and made his way to the bathroom. The phone rang almost immediately. Moaning with displeasure he turned back as he wondered who would ring so early, and checked his watch. It showed the exact time, two o'clock in the afternoon. "Hmm," he said out loud and looked at the caller ID: Alina. He eyed the phone for a few seconds without touching it, as if it might infect him. Finally, he picked it up and answered. A soft female voice sang the word, "Hello," sweetly from afar.

They met a few hours later. Alina was wearing a wavy red dress, her hair had been trimmed and shone as brightly as the sun. Sergei saw her in the distance as he stood by the entrance to the café.

"Hi, why are you so sad? You haven't written to or called me for a week," Alina reproached him.

Sergei wanted to say something in his defence, but only smiled easily. They decided not to go inside but to walk in the fresh air. The conversation did not gel to begin with; he was silent and immersed in his own thoughts. His companion waited for him to finally wake up. They walked for a few blocks before reaching the Botanical Gardens. The shadow of a chestnut tree concealed a sweet moist coolness, the pair sat on a bench underneath it and Sergei smiled easily again as the Kyiv air wrapped around him like a blanket.

He had noted long ago that the Ukrainian capital had one unique feature. Other cities might flaunt their ancient architecture, and still others their modern skyscrapers, while other cities might stream with tourists, however, Kyiv always had a quality that was incalculable, sincere, and free. This city was not, it seemed, composed of arterial roads, the skeletons of buildings or uncluttered open squares; it had all of these elements, but its main quality was its spirituality.

Sergei was still extremely stressed, but his anxiety decreased as each minute passed. He began to tell Alina about his childhood. How he was different from his brother; even in his external appearance.

"People asked my parents where they had got such a handsome son," he grinned.

"Why, do you think you are so different from Anton?" she asked suddenly.

"Why? We are even different visually. He's curly haired, and me." Sergei patted his hair.

"Yes, but you didn't answer the question, why?" Alina persisted.

"Well, what can I say," Sergei said and paused abruptly. He had so often made a distinction between himself and his brother that he had forgotten where it all began. "Well, it's all about…" He tried to compose a sentence, but all that came to mind was an often hackneyed phrase, "He paints pictures and I don't," he blurted, breaking off as if he had said something important.

"So, start painting, what's the problem?" said Alina, continuing to grill him.

"Me? I've never tried to," Sergei muttered.

"It's easy. You just release your hand and let it paint," Alina advised him.

Sergei looked at her, as if seeing her for the first time. He looked at her face silently and thought that life's motions were incomprehensible. Only yesterday he had been suffering because of broken love and the betrayal of a woman; her constant excuses and changing mind. This morning he had pondered how she manipulated men because she was bored in her marriage. She wanted variety and men falling for her, and uttering ardent

168

words. This verbal game of words and feelings had reached Sergei. However, he now thought that Kolia's sterility had been dreamed up in a moment by Yulia. She had told all her lovers that tale and supported that myth. The realisation of this fact blew his mind. He suddenly understood that his difference from his brother was perhaps not so profound. Certainly nothing emerged as he tried to identify that distinction in words.

"If I paint what will become of it now?" Sergei asked her in a childlike manner.

She smiled. Her eyes were transformed into two thin lines, making her yet more beautiful. She placed her hand in his palm and he felt the softness and warmth of her skin.

"All things may happen then, everything or nothing," said Alina enigmatically as she stopped smiling.

Chapter Nineteen

Five hundred people from Debaltsevo and Rosijska Vesna, which were previously under the control of Kyiv, have become volunteers in the army of Novorossiya. The head of the DPR, Aleksandr Zakharchenko, said that the new recruits were preparing to hold Ukraine's illegal military formations to account for the ruin of their small homeland. "There are insufficient forces on the Ukrainian side to defeat us militarily, so they are increasing pressure on the political, military and diplomatic fronts," he added.

From an item on the Russkaia Vesna site, 27.02.2015

Artist awoke that morning in a terrific mood and summoned the nurse with only one request; he needed to telephone his father to tell him everything was okay, he had almost recovered. The nurse, an attractive twenty-five year old woman, stood before him like a student before their teacher during an exam. She tried to force something out, but the words stuck in her throat. Finally, she collected her strength and slowly broke the news to him, "Your father was killed yesterday. He asked to go on a reconnaissance mission near the town of Shchastia and they all caught it. He stumbled on a tripwire. There are only a few pieces of the body left."

Artist looked at the pure, beautiful face of the nurse, unable to believe what she had said. "Leave me alone," he said, turning slowly and painfully on to his side.

Warm rays of summer sunshine stole furtively through the narrow entrance of the tent and were cut delicately by dust-motes hanging in the air. A fly continued its aerobatics over the bed, landing and taking off from the blanket repeatedly. The chair, like a mute partner in some conversation, looked away from the person lying beneath the picture, who was curled up and who groaned ever more loudly as the minutes passed; as if trying to extract a bullet that had caused him excruciating pain, tearing his innards and searing him like fire. His nerves were in shreds and his body spasmed painfully and involuntarily. He tried to extract that bullet which no surgeon's knife could reach, for it lay in the most sensitive part of the human anatomy, the soul.

The militants' camp woke and someone wandered to a small river nearby. Some soldiers laughed and smoked near the fragmented remnants of a burned out T 72. A wailing that sounded ever louder and inhuman, like the cry of a wounded whale, echoed from Artist's tent.

One month had passed since the loss of his father. The end of the war was approaching. The military formations of Novorossiya had driven back the Ukrainian army and had done so with the help of thousands of regular Russian troops, Russian supplied arms, and hundreds of Russian armoured vehicles. They occupied half of Donbas, comprising part of the Donetsk and Luhansk provinces. Walls were being built along the border by both sides. A police force and courts appeared in the DPR and LPR. These territories were officially termed by Russia as the Novorossiyskij Autonomous District of Ukraine, but they were under the control of the heads of the DPR and LPR; they, in their turn, were controlled by the Kremlin's special services.

The first winter of the war came and Artist was travelling with a column of tanks and armoured vehicles. Ahead of them soldiers leaped out of a KRAZ military truck, then someone unloaded rations. Military operations had almost ceased at this point. The border area between the Russian proxies and Ukrainian military remained in place and had, indeed, been strengthened by both sides. It was unclear what would happen in the spring. A truce had been officially agreed, but they were preparing for war, so new militia forces appeared in the camp and Artist was summoned to the headquarters.

People were bustling near the commander's tent, including a few of his acquaintances. He turned to one of them. "Vitalii, pal, what's going on?"

"Eh, bro, they don't want to give us our cash. They promised us four hundred dollars last month, but no one's seen it," Vitalii replied. He was a chunky man of about thirty years of age.

People talked, there were muffled expletives. Shots sounded in the distance.

"The Ukropi just can't relax," muttered Vitalii irritably, merging back into the crowd.

Artist entered the tent. The moustachioed battalion commander leaned over the map. Someone dozed in the corner. Some Russian officers sat at the table and wrote something.

"Ah, Anton, come in," said the commander before he could salute him. Artist entered the interior of the tent and stood by the table while the commander continued to draw something on the map, but a minute later one of the Russian officers looked up from his sheet of paper. "What do that rabble gathered near the entrance want?" he asked the commander. The commander hesitated, not knowing what to say, and an awkward pause followed.

"Look, I explained it to you in the Russian language last time. Those who are owed the most in wage arrears should be moved to the front of any hot spot. Don't you know what's needed to economise?" the Russian said with unexpected coarseness.

"Dmitrij Nikola…" the battalion commander wanted to say something, but before he had even finished the officer's name he was cut short with a torrent of foul language.

"Shut up, you never understood what was needed from the first moment onwards. You'll go to the front yourself, I'll teach you some discipline, I'll bury you sharpish, do you think you're irreplaceable?" The Russian spoke in a calm, sepulchral

172

voice, but his tone was menacing.

A tense silence hung within the tent. The Russian officer looked in the direction of the commander, as if he were looking at no one. The commander, confused, aimlessly directed his pencil over the map. On that day Artist left his position as unit commander and joined the security division. He had explained to his colleagues that he was tired of everything on earth, but he no longer knew where to look for those signs that had once, he believed, directed his destiny.

Rows of bales of military uniforms stood in a large hangar. A heap of boots loomed further inside the structure. Still deeper inside the hangar were boxes with canned foods. Almost no one came here except when driving in to unload a vehicle and then leaving. Artist strode around the hangar until it was dark, as if wanting to trample down his thoughts. The mine, Liuba and the children hovered before his eyes. His hands occasionally rose, as if wanting to pluck some substantial object from the air that only he could see, but they sank into a void and found no support; like a climber who makes a wrong move and cannot cling on to a ledge.

Artist heard later that a mishap had occurred regarding Father Vladimir, the priest who had helped him conquer his addiction to gambling. He had allegedly begun to speak out openly against the militia who stole from his parishioners. They had in turn promised to 'wring the priest's neck'. Artist did not know who had made the threat, so he went on leave and journeyed to the priest in Rovenky. He requisitioned a free truck to travel to his hometown and left the camp, heading south on a December morning. He decided to visit his mother first.

The familiar residential building loomed over the Chernigovskii residential district. He ascended to the second floor and the door, upholstered in brown leatherette, he knew so well. His mother answered when he knocked. How she had aged. Anton had not seen her for several months, but it seemed that years had passed.

"Son, you're alive," she said, stretching her hands towards him and looking at him. They embraced for half a minute. "Come in, you're surely tired, you must rest." She looked at her son and tears began to creep from her eyes.

"I can't stop long, Mum, I've got stuff to sort out here," he said, and flopped into an armchair.

Nothing had changed in the apartment. As usual, her three cats sullied everything in the apartment among the old furniture. Something new; a photograph of his father in a black frame. He froze for a minute, clenching his jaw after he saw the image of his father.

"Your father has ceased suffering, God rest his soul," his mother said.

Anton turned to look at her and she looked a little to the side. Her voice had sounded level, as if she talked about someone she barely knew. "Why do you talk like that, don't you regret his loss?" Anton asked.

His mother sobbed, clearly not wanting to answer. "I cried of course, and I grieved, and it hurt that he died like that," she said and fell silent. It was obvious she was preparing to say something negative about his father. However, she did not dare utter whatever it was in front of her son.

"What is it Mum? What's up?" Anton saw her agitation and had a vague idea of what his mother would say. His father did not love her, he partied and boozed, and his death was not a tragedy for her.

"It's nothing son, I'll make you some tea now." She broke off the conversation and rushed into the kitchen, covering her face with her hand.

Anton stared after her, dumbfounded. His internal agony at the loss of his father was so overwhelming that it seemed to fill the whole world, yet his own mother apparently was not hurt with grief for him. Yes, the old man had been a difficult character, but he and Anton's mother had lived together for over thirty years.

Anton began pacing the room in frustration, seething inwardly. His mother deliberately lingered in the kitchen, not wanting to come out to face her son. This carried on for about five minutes until Anton stopped by a wall adorned by one of his pictures. He paused to look at his work, which depicted a pitcher with blue flowers. He looked at the brush strokes and they seemed foreign to him. The painting had been executed a long time ago, before he had worked at the mine. He looked at the image and realised it had been painted by someone else.

"After lunch Liuba will bring the children to visit, you'll see your family," his mother said, popping back into the room for a second to defuse the situation before returning to brew the tea.

"Mum, I've only come here to deal with one thing," he replied angrily, sitting in the chair and closing his eyes.

His mother came into the room and clattered the crockery together, rather expressively. Then she hurried off to make the bread and butter. Her son smelled that domestic fragrance and immersed himself slowly in a dream. A dream where he again felt himself to be a little boy sitting at the table. His pencil glided over the canvas, sketching, and his father standing near him. He stood so quietly that the son did not hear him, he only realised his father was nearby when Anatolii placed a hand on his shoulder.

"Eat, son," his mother said, placing a hand on his shoulder and waking him.

Later that day Anton stood near the church and talked with the priest. Father Vladimir was a good deal frailer now, he leaned on a stick and his body seemed bent with the earth's gravitational pull, making it appear stooped. The priest said something, raised his hand and pointed towards the church, then towards the militant's base. Anton listened to him for a long time without making a sound. If someone standing nearby had looked at them it would have appeared the two men were silent; their hands occasionally moved as if they were enchanted and chained to one place. Anton briskly walked away from the priest's side and headed towards the local militia base. No one saw him after that, he disappeared as if he had fallen into the mine workings.

One month later Sergei again received a text message from Liuba asking for his help to locate Anton. He was sitting in a café and the waiter had just brought him the second course, but the food stuck in his throat. He phoned Zbigniew, still in shock, and begged him to help. He promised to do something and, furthermore, he was meeting with the leaders of the Anton's battalion on the following day.

Sergei settled in Kyiv and rented an apartment. On a day early in March he heard a knock on his door. When he opened it he saw a delivery service man with a package, one metre square, wrapped in paper. "This package is for you, along with a letter," said the man and stood, waiting for a tip. After paying, Sergei went to his large, brown desk and opened the letter, which was from Zbigniew. It told him that he had been unable to locate Anton. The battalion command knew nothing about his whereabouts; they had simply handed him the items from Anton's tent.

Sergei opened the package with trembling hands. It was a painting. He was afraid as he slowly revealed the canvas. His interior world, which was seemingly so carefully constructed, tore like fragile, antique paper. He positioned the picture on a chair and stepped back. His whole body trembled as he saw a grey, autumnal Steppe field extended across the canvas, a small

176

hill broke the level perspective towards the horizon and the plane beyond it faded into grey space, several trees protruded on the left, a shaggy bush loomed on the right, there was a dirt road indented with two wheel lines and two people were sitting in the middle of it. They were so tired of walking their heads hung downwards and they were apparently taking about something; about a universe which belonged to them alone. This was their world and it would be difficult for a stranger to penetrate. It had its own physical and mechanical laws. Some unknown person's desire meant that these two kindred spirits had closed this world, and it remained only for them. However, just ten metres away, a man steps towards them. He steps confidently forward, though his face shows signs of struggle, doubts, fear and hope. The third man strides towards them from the horizon and is poised a few steps away. He seemingly does not understand this pair, has not lived their life and accepted them in his heart. Only a few metres separate them.

The right hand side of the canvas is inscribed with the words 'Family, Anton Nedelkov, April 2014'.

Sergei sat on a chair across from the painting. Everything in his spirit turned to stone. He could neither weep nor speak. He approached the computer and opened an email service to create a new profile. In the box for the profile's name he typed one word slowly, as if completing the missing, still un-walked steps on the canvas: Artist.

Glossary

Banderites - the followers of WW2 Ukrainian nationalist leader Stepan Bandera
Oranges - The politicians who came to power following the Orange Revolution of 2004-2005
Potomu Chto nelzya byt na svete krasyvoj takoj - a Russian pop song
Slava Ukraiini - a patriotic Ukrainian salutation cum battle cry which translates as "Glory to Ukraine!"

Also available from Kalyna Language Press

Episodic Memory by Liubov Holota

Winner of the 2008 Shevchenko Prize

Episodic Memory, published in Ukraine in 2007, is the story of a young girl, Sofia, growing up in a Ukrainian village, and her return, as an adult, to be at her dying mother's bedside. While staying in her parent's house after the funeral, she is haunted by memories of a vanished world where Gypsies sang their way over the Steppe and the post man, a KGB informer, hurled the mail at their gatepost as his wagon hurtled past.

Raven's Way by Vasyl Shkliar

Winner of the 2011 Shevchenko Prize

In 1921, after four years of war, the Bolsheviks conquer Ukraine, but Raven and Veremii hide in the forest with other Cossacks and continue their struggle. When Veremii dies in battle, the communists secretly follow the burial party, but when they dig up the coffin they find a cryptic note instead of a corpse.

The novel brings to light the desperate resistance of a guerrilla army that fought until 1926, conducting daring attacks on Soviet forces and concealing themselves in underground lairs that could hold hundreds of Cossacks.

Kaharlyk by Oleh Shynkarenko

The novel began on Facebook as a series of bulletins from an alternative reality, and is written entirely in blocks of 100 words. It is set in Ukraine after a war with Russia. A man has lost his memory because the Russian army have used his brain to control military satellites. He regains consciousness in a mysterious hospital-like building and begins a pilgrimage to find his past. He journeys to Kaharlyk, a town where time has stood still following the testing of an experimental weapon.

The book is an Odyssey as magical as Alice's tumble through the looking glass or Gulliver's first footprints on the sands of Lilliput.

www.kalynalanguagepress.com